Twelve Branches

Stories from St. Paul

NORA MURPHY
JOANNA RAWSON
JULIA KLATT SINGER
DIEGO VÁZQUEZ, JR.

COFFEE HOUSE PRESS

2003

Coffee House Press books are available to the trade through our primary distributor, Consortium Book Sales & Distribution, 1045 Westgate Drive, St. Paul, MN 55114. For personal orders, catalogs, or other information, write to: Coffee House Press, 27 North Fourth Street, Suite 400, Minneapolis, MN 55401.

Coffee House Press is an independent nonprofit literary publisher. This book received special project support from the the Irwin Andrew Porter Foundation. Funds from a general operating support grant from the Minnesota State Arts Board, through an appropriation by the Minnesota State Legislature and a grant from the National Endowment for the Arts, also contributed to this project. All our books are made possible through the generous support of grants and gifts from many foundations, corporate giving programs, individuals, and through state and federal support.

To you and our many readers across the country,
we send our thanks for your continuing support.

Good books are brewing at coffeehousepress.org

~

Library of Congress CIP Information

Twelve branches : stories from St. Paul / by Nora Murphy,
p. cm
ISBN 1-56689-140-X
1. Short stories, American—Minnesota—St. Paul 2. St. Paul (Minn.)—Fiction
I. Murphy, Nora; Rawson, Joanna; Singer, Julia Klatt; Vázquez Jr., Diego

PS 572.S255T88 2003
813'.01089776581—DC21

2003041221

First edition | First printing
1 2 3 4 5 6 7 8 9

Printed in Canada

Contents

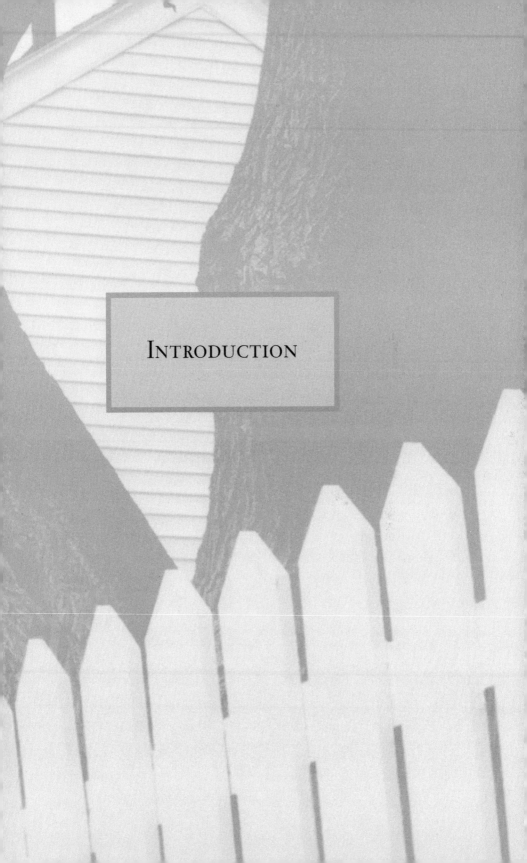

INTRODUCTION

Introduction

How many times have you heard someone say that "if you want to kill a good idea, just assign it to a committee"? The story I like best is how the camel was conceived by a committee set up by a higher power charged with designing a horse. Nevertheless, I was actually looking forward to chairing the program committee of The Friends of the St. Paul Public Library—a position I assumed in June, 1999.

Why? Well, I guess you could say there comes a time when it just feels right. Under the aegis of The Friends, a truly marvelous group of volunteers had joined the program committee. It was a diverse, multiethnic group of neighborhood activists, writers, professors, library staff, administrators, and Friends board members. Although our backgrounds were different, we were all united by a desire to develop creative endeavors that would increase use of the St. Paul Public Library through creative cultural programming.

The group's energy was infectious, and many said they even looked forward to attending our meetings! Under the guidance of Friends staff, and with the enthusiastic cooperation of the library staff, a number of innovative and creative cultural programs were developed and implemented. Our efforts were recognized when the American Library Association awarded the Marshall Cavendish Excellence in Programming Award to The Friends in 2001.

The concept for *Twelve Branches: Stories from St. Paul* arose at a summer meeting in 2001 devoted to generating ideas for future programs. The committee wanted a project that would coincide with the reopening of our Central Library following two years of renovations, and at the same time would reconnect the vast array of library services to the broadest number of potential users throughout St. Paul.

As usual, suggestions bounced off the walls in the free-spirited, free-wheeling manner that characterized our meetings. As chair, I was last to speak, which gave me the advantage of hearing all the wonderful ideas preceding mine. All were excellent, and as I listened, I wondered if we could incorporate all of them into one program. Fortunately, when my turn came, it hit me! Why don't we chain-write a book, asking the community members living in each of the twelve branch library neighborhoods to help us create the stories and characters?

It was a notion that struck a chord with the committee. Within minutes suggestions were added to the original thought, revising, expanding, and affirming the idea that this would be the "mother of all cultural programs" for our committee and for the library system.

And so our journey began. After many interesting and always stimulating meetings, what ultimately emerged retained the fundamental components that the committee had sought. In *Twelve Branches,* the four authors take ordinary voices and weave them into stories describing the streets and neighborhoods, people and places of St. Paul—stories that give an eloquent tone to the qualities that set our city apart and capture the unwary with its charms. As a result, thanks to the efforts of many community members and these wonderfully crafted stories, you will soon discover what long-time residents have known for years—but have been reluctant to share—that St. Paul is indeed a wonderful place to live, to work, and to grow.

That this was accomplished by committee makes it all the more remarkable. For this I would like to acknowledge and thank the members of The Friends' program committee: Amy Adams, Julia Adams, Roger Barr, Dorothea Burns, Gilbert de la O, Daniel Gabriel, Anita Gonzalez, Eleanor Heginbotham, Gloria Kumagai, George Latimer, Perrin Lilly, Steve Nelson, Alice Neve, Karen Smith, Vallay Varro, Elaine Wagner, Debbie Willms, and Jym Wroblewski.

Very special thanks go to The Friends of the St. Paul Public Library staff: Andrea Moerer, Eric Watson, and Stewart J. Wilson. Additional thanks are extended to: Carole Williams and the staff of the St. Paul Public Library, especially all of the branch supervisors; Chris Fischbach, Allan Kornblum, and all of the staff at Coffee House Press; The Friends' Board of Trustees; and Peter Pearson, President of The Friends. I want to express my most sincere appreciation for their unwavering support and encouragement.

Special recognition is given to the Anna M. Heilmaier Charitable Foundation, Target Stores, *St. Paul Pioneer Press,* and the Irwin Andrew Porter Foundation for their financial and sponsorship support. And to others not named, including all of the book's community contributors, our debts to you are gratefully acknowledged.

Very special recognition and much thanks to the authors: Nora Murphy, Joise Rawson, Julia Klatt Singer, and Diego Vázquez for understanding our dream, bringing it to life, and sharing the secrets of St. Paul with the world.

Marvin R. Anderson
Chair, Friends of the St. Paul Public Library Program Committee
December, 2002

THE FIRST TIME
I SAW ST. PAUL

The First Time I Saw St. Paul

DIEGO VÁZQUEZ, JR.

Riverview

I hear the news at the airport. The entire block on Dayton's Bluff where Paul's Bar sits has exploded from a gas leak. The radio calls it an enormous explosion. This news destroys the innocence of the day. I am at the Minneapolis-St. Paul airport. I was at Paul's Bar less than thirty minutes ago, and all I see now is a girl holding red flowers and a woman who looks like Janine holding the little girl's hand as they start to cross the intersection. The light is against them but I am driving the only car stopped at this crossroad. No one else to honk a horn, Chicago style, or to hit the gas and scare them into running fast across the street. There is no traffic anywhere else in the world other than this woman and child crossing the street on my green light. They don't care. They know I will not move. They laugh with each other and disappear. I have just left Paul's Bar. The light changes twice before I drive away. I head for the airport to catch a flight to Anchorage.

The buildings on the bluff are burning and all I have left is the Janine look-alike crossing the street with the girl holding red flowers. I find a phone and dial the number for Paul's Bar. I call Janine's house. She is the early shift bar-keep at Paul's. The television inside the bar broadcasts more news of the explosion and I want to feel Janine handing me a cold beer early in the morning before I hop a flight for my trip to the Kuparak oil field. I want her to ask me again, "What is a Kuparak? Why do you go all the way to Alaska to work? How can you stand to be there for three months at a time?" I want her to ask me seven thousand questions as she pours me another cold one. No one answers the phone. The news reports are still sketchy as my flight approaches. I have never missed a shift change since I got transferred to the Pingo site on Kuparak. I will not miss my flight.

I raise my voice to the bartender and ask for another beer, quickly. I don't notice if the bartender is a man or a woman. I don't even notice the other people in the bar. But I begin to talk to anyone and no one at the same time. I simply begin talking out loud for anyone to listen. I say "Janine" loudly, over the bar crowd conversation. I say that she was a friend who served me freebies at Paul's. And that we laughed a lot together. That she has a five-year-old daughter from a psycho gunrunner who was doing time in St. Cloud at the state nuthouse. Janine had been pouring drinks for a long time at the first Paul's Bar on Front Street but had recently started filling in at the second Paul's on Dayton's Bluff. The gas leak had her name on it.

I think about driving away from the bluff. I want to know that I can return from my long stretch of time on the Arctic oil fields and walk back into Paul's Bar and smile and feel happy while I drink a cold morning beer in a quiet neighborhood bar. The airport announces an hour delay for my flight. I order another beer and walk to the phone to call Nora.

I start thinking about the first time my mother and I came to St. Paul and how we first met Nora. I call her office in downtown St. Paul and beg her to send me more information about the explosion. Nora has been a fixture in our life ever since that first night. She has always helped me when I felt that there was no direction in this whole earth catalog. Her vision has so often reappeared to me as a source of great comfort and much warmth. With Nora I discovered that I could love another woman as if she too were my mother.

The first time I saw St. Paul I was almost sleeping on my mother's lap. The train rumbling along the river in darkness and the sudden lights of the city kept me awake. I moved my head onto my mother's shoulder. She nervously ran her fingers through my hair. I was at peace, but I knew the tranquil ride was about to end.

My mother whispered, "Ay, que chingadera. Things are so screwed up. Mi'jo, Jimmy, we are almost there."

We had boarded the train in Chicago earlier in the day. We were planning to return home to El Paso, but my uncle Pancho convinced my mom to check out the opportunities in the Midwest. My mother was a single girl with big dreams and a small boy. The "single" part was recent. She was a war widow and I was the son of a dead soldier. I was seven years old and still young enough to rest my head on her lap and fall asleep between her legs.

My father, Pablo Mistral de Sanchez, came back from World War II after the siege of Guadalcanal. In El Paso he was a war hero. There was not a bar or a pretty lady in town who would not offer their rewards for a job well done and for coming home alive. Seven years after the battle was over he was still shell-shocked from that besieged island. I was four years old when he first got very sick. I was five when we said good-bye to him at the VA hospital in Lubbock. He was twenty-nine. His final message to me had three "don'ts" in it: "Don't ever touch a woman in an unkind way. Don't ever hit a woman. Don't ever go to war. Son, follow these three don'ts and the good life will be yours. Don't ever go to war and the others will take care of themselves. Don't ever go to war. If war ever comes near you, run. And make everyone you love run with you."

The St. Paul train depot stood big and strong. A woman who had been sitting near us on the train walked off with us. She and my mother had spoken briefly during the ride. But each time they had started to talk in depth something got in the way. She walked off the train with us and began speaking to my mother. "Hello, my name is Nora. Nora O'Connell. I was born in St. Paul but never really spent much time here because my parents were always on the move." Nora appeared to be about the same age as my mother. They looked pretty together. She continued, "My mom was born in Long Prairie and my dad, well we never were quite sure where he came from. He mostly just said he was 'Irish. Fresh off the boat.' He was always changing the story about which part of Ireland. When I was younger we followed a lot of the farm work during the season. Are you coming here for the season? I hope not. The work is so tough and so long and the pay is so low. The season is ending now anyway. Do you have family here in town?"

My mother stared at Nora for a long time. Nora continued talking. "I am sorry if I sound so nosy but I have not been able to take my eyes off of the two of you. Is it just you two? Are you married? War widow maybe? I am. He died before coming back home. We didn't get married before he left, but I am still his widow in my heart. It was a long time ago. Now I'm twenty-six and I have yet to get married. I am sorry for telling you all of this, I just feel connected to you for some odd reason. Listen, please take my name and number. I work at the downtown library. The main one. It's big, you can't miss it. But I am hard to find because I am the research librarian. I am always hidden in some dark corner. I will give you the phone number. I hope you don't find me strange, but I just feel like it would be good to get to know the two of you. Do you have a place to stay?"

I smiled at Nora and then looked at my mother. She was forming long sentences with her eyes and I could almost read each one.

"Well. Nora. You are quite a surprise. My son, Jimmy and I . . . Oh, my name is Olivia Mistral, Olivia Mistral from El Paso, Texas. Jimmy and I were in Chicago for a few months. I lost my husband two years ago. He was in the war too, so I guess I am also a war widow. You know, nowadays I just feel angry, not sad. We have been thinking about returning to Texas because school has already started, but we might just stay here and start brand new. I have a brother who lives here. He has been telling me for the past two years that I need to come out and start brand new with Jimmy. My brother and my sister-in-law and my nieces and nephews live on the West Side of St. Paul. He keeps telling me not to confuse it with a place called West St. Paul. Do you know this area he talks about?"

Nora was surrounded with a smile. "Yes, dear. I live near the West Side. It's the favorite spot for all the Latinos who settle down in St. Paul. My dead soldier was Gilbert Rodriquez from 'la West Side.' I think the first thing that made Gilbert take notice of me is that I can speak fluent Spanish. And not the Spain Español but like he said, 'the real Mexican Spanish de Tejas.'" Her voice fell soft and quiet. We stood and stared, quietly, at each other.

The smells of downtown St. Paul reminded me of wintertime in El Paso. It was early September and the night sky was wide. The streets of this new city were dark and wet with lights bigger than my Texas hometown lights. But it felt much smaller than Chicago, and cleaner. I liked the size of this city. St. Paul was falling on our shoulders and this Irish angel, Nora O'Connell, was holding us up.

My mother had changed her mind countless times while we were in Chicago. She did not want to return to the Southwest. At the last minute she read about the Empire Builder route. It started in Chicago and went through St. Paul on the way to the west coast and Seattle. Her older brother Pancho, who lived in St. Paul, had always taken care of us. Even when my dad was alive and killing his war memories in all those bars and inside the skirts of all those friendly women, tío Pancho always held us close to his heart. The whole family did: tía Lydia who suffered from epilepsy and my older cousins, Nicky, Cynthia, and Martha. Tío had told my mother to call him if she decided to come to St. Paul. We were so late getting to the train in Chicago that my mother didn't have time to let anyone know that we finally were coming into town.

"Nora, thank you for your kindness. Can you give us directions to the West Side? Is it far from here? Can Jimmy and I catch a cab? I think it would be fun to surprise everyone at my brother's house. We are used to surprises at my mom's house in El Paso. Everything in our family in Texas runs through my mom's house. She is grandmother to all. She might be abuelita to just about everyone else, but she is still my mom. When my dad died she kept the bakeries going. I come from a long line of bakers. Oh, I am sorry. I am just missing her so much right now."

My mom felt like crying but she had toughened up considerably during the previous two years. We had been in Chicago because she had followed a boyfriend there. He had promised her heaven but when we got there it was pure hell. First thing we found out was that he was still very much married with a bunch of kids. He was a baker's goods salesman who sold flour for the big Midwestern mills. He first met my mother at my grandfather's bakery in El Paso. The bum had been in Texas setting up a flour distribution system from the Minneapolis mills by the railcar load to small Texas cities. I don't remember much about the early stage in their relationship, just that my mother and I were on the Southern Pacific to Chicago to try a new exciting life. He had a room for us in the ugliest and scariest part of a city that I have ever lived in. It was a sub-basement room and it stunk like a muddy river. He waited until we arrived in Chicago to tell her his new story. The jerk was just getting out of his marriage and as soon as it was over he would take care of us. My mother immediately went to work in one of the Mexican bakeries and worked for eight weeks. Just long enough for us to get money to leave town.

My mother was walking so fast that the sidewalk moved as she held my hand and we headed toward the train depot in Chicago. The jerk was screaming at us from across the street but Mom continued walking with her little Jimmy tightly holding her hand. We could hear the screaming blocks away, but the bum never chased after us. My mom whispered to herself over and over, "Jimmy, I will never let you be a man like that. Never." Our exodus started with the walls of the buildings bulging with giant spiders and fat snakes swirling along the edges of darkness in long alleys, so the footsteps that my mother and I took were fast and wild. We had to navigate toward safety. I searched the streets for a friend but we were strangers in the Windy City. We carried few belongings. I held a bag filled with coloring books, crayons, and *Archie* and *Jughead* comic books. I also had some paper and pencils. I used to invent words and then I would ask my mom to try and spell them. I saw the Texas desert in my mom's footsteps and I knew that we would soon be wrapped in the shelter of a big sun rising across a large sky.

That first night in St. Paul was magic for the three of us. We set out on a long walk outside of the train depot and Nora continued to enchant us with her stories. "Listen. I can give you a ride to your brother's house if you don't mind. Like I said, I live right there. Well, almost right there. I live in place called Lillydale. So do you want to know why I was in Chicago?"

Nora really wanted to tell us why she had been in Chicago. When we got to her car the conversation turned quickly to what a nice car she drove, but after we were inside the car she again wanted to talk about her recent trip.

I interrupted Nora because she acted older than my mom. "Nora, how old are you, really?"

My mother and Nora both laughed. My mom, still laughing, told me, "Mi'jo you don't ask those things of a lady. Besides, she already told us. And if she wants to let you know her real age she will tell you. Ay Jimmy, sometimes you are so full of surprises."

I wasn't afraid of the darkness of this new city. The sky was cold but the two women walking in front of me were the warmest bodies in the universe. My mother was brown-haired and tall with sea-green eyes. She liked saying that they were sea-green. I told her that they were the color of Crayola light green. Nora was red-haired, freckled, wore polka dots, and stared at us with bright blue eyes. I did not know what color blue to call them because they were so bright it was almost hard to look directly at them. We saw a falling star. We started looking for another one. We wished for a better life in a sky that was being so kind on that first night, in a city named for a saint whose cathedral on a hill could be seen from everywhere. The mystery of our new adventure arrived in a wide continuous song of peace from a town that I did not yet know, but wanted to call my own.

Over the years it seems that I only call Nora when I need information. I have been spoiled with the easy access to her research. During the draft for the war in Vietnam she gave me tons of memos and policy pieces on how best to avoid the draft. Both she and my mother always reminded me of my father's words, "Son, mi'jo, Jimmy, run from war, boy. And if it comes close to you, run from it with all the people you love." Through the years the quotes would get longer, more philosophical, and include more people.

I ran with the best of the dodgers. I went to the west coast and registered for the draft 1800 miles away from my real home in St. Paul. My first draft board was in West Hollywood, California. I told everyone that while I was cutting out on the draft I might as well stay in Hollywood and get discovered. I discovered Cesar Chavez and the United Farm Workers Organizing Committee instead. I volunteered. I discovered the Movimiento Estudiantil Chicano de Aztlan, MEChA. I discovered the anti-war movement and the East L.A. riots where my hero, Ruben Salazar, originally from my hometown of El Paso, was killed by a tear gas canister to the head at the Silver Dollar Saloon. I discovered that running from the draft had not kept me out of the war. And two years later, in a federal magistrate office in Jacksonville, Florida, my running from the war days came to a startling end as I lifted my right hand in a pledge to the u.s. Army. I discovered boot camp in Fort Knox, Kentucky, Advanced Infantry Training in Fort Bliss, Texas, and the tears from two angels in St. Paul who told me that all their prayers were devoted to me to be kept out of the war. After Fort Bliss, I discovered why my dad told me to run from war. And I will always wish I had not made this discovery. I am grateful that I have maintained vigilance on two out of the three "don'ts."

My mother has never left St. Paul. We found a very good life in Minnesota, but I hardly ever stayed long enough to call it home. In the early years I would go back and forth to live with my grandmother in El Paso. I finished most of my elementary schooling in Texas. Then I got sent briefly to a Jesuit high school. Fortunately for me, the nightmare with the Society of Jesus did not last long. Jesuit priests and brothers were just too cruel and violent for me to accept their calling. I came back to finish my high school career at Humboldt High in St. Paul. I left town on graduation day and eventually wound up at Florida State University in Tallahassee. I did not qualify for a student deferment from the lottery draft. My battle to run away from the war failed. Through it all my two angels in St. Paul were the ones who spoiled me the most. My mother and Nora now live together. They have for a long time.

Twenty-seven days after leaving the airport bar and my mumblings about the explosion on Dayton's Bluff, I get confirmation that Janine will never again pour a tap at the now nonexistent Paul's Bar. Nora has sent me a full packet of news clippings about the explosion. The red flowers left on the street are unforgivable reminders that I left too soon. All the bodies have been recovered and buried. The tundra is not a comfort. I am too far away from the real world. I want to go back. But I have never missed a shift change. I weep in the arctic.

And twenty-seven days after again leaving St. Paul I am sad because Janine will never again laugh with me and ask me seven thousand questions about my work in Alaska. Never again will she tell me that I am one funny Chicano. Like a butterfly. A Latino mariposa. Never again can I tell Janine that the Westsiders are so different from my truly real vatos locos de Tejas. Never again to compare the colors of hope under the bright sky filled with cold beer and delirious dreams of stars falling as if they can drop peace onto this planet.

Chicken

Chicken

JULIA KLATT SINGER
Rice Street

It was Ada and Winifred's job to pick rocks—the best crop those forty acres ever had. A job that started in early spring, after the plow pried open the earth (or tried to) and lasted until long after the harvest. They picked until the fields froze or were buried in snow. Their fingers went numb, knuckles raw, Thanksgiving came, and Christmas was just around the corner. Fall was not a season here, but a few crisp days scattered amongst a month or two of cold, gray, fading light days. The mice had more luck than them, leaving the fields soon after the corn and wheat were harvested. Winter was the only season they didn't pick rocks.

They remember going to town on Christmas Eve, their daddy hitching the team to a sleigh and riding with blankets folded so the holes didn't show, to church. Ada hated the bitter ride in the sleigh, hated sitting still on the wooden pew, hated the way the preacher spoke of the graciousness of God—what had God given them of late? Crops so thin they all went to bed hungry, sick little baby Hannah, the wolves that stalked them from the edge of the fields? The preacher said that only those deserving got the goods. Got Jesus as their savior. Got everlasting life—why you'd want that Ada didn't know. One life was hungry and long and hard enough.

And then there were the old ladies singing like creaky porch swings. The old men snorting and hacking up phlegm. It was enough to drive Ada batty. The only pleasant thing was the faint smell of her mother's talcum powder, and the feel of her mother's lap when she put her head on it to sleep.

Winifred said *be grateful and sit still* whenever Ada scoffed and fidgeted. After the service there was a potato pancake dinner and all the needy children were lined up and handed a present and a small sack of candy. The preacher's wife and snotty little girl dressed in new shoes and pretty new dresses did the handing out.

Ada knew, after she was given a stuffed baby chick with "Jesus Loves You" embroidered on its wing, that she was going to stop going to church altogether. Winifred received a blue-eyed baby doll with a glass head, real hair, a pillow-soft body, and a change of clothes. Ada could see where in God's pecking order she stood. So she stayed home from then on and cleaned house and cooked dinner—some years just biscuits and gravy, others glazed ham or a roast chicken.

Only Christians would rejoice in the dead of winter and nail somebody to a cross in the springtime, thought Ada. She could never forgive them for that. Spring was her favorite time of year, what with the world greening up: moss, then grasses and dandelions, then the currant bushes and honeysuckle, culminating with the trees' leaves opening like the wings of butterflies. She loved everything about spring. She loved the mud vacations from school when the roads became impassable, the ruts too deep for the school bus to travel through. Those were the best days to hunt for mushrooms, duck eggs, tadpoles, and wild turkeys. On days like those, being too soon to pick rocks, she even believed there might be a god.

~

"Unless you're chicken . . . " Conway said, folding his hands on the stainless steel counter, revealing nothing. His left eyebrow twitched slightly, indicating something, although Maple wasn't exactly sure what it was. His hands were huge, she noticed, almost the size of a salad plate. Later she would find that those hands could fix the most delicate things: the workings of a pocket watch, the setting of a ring, and no sliver was too small for him to slip from beneath the skin.

"I've *been* on a bike before, Mr. Milton. If you think I'm afraid to ride with you, then you don't know me very well."

"*Conway*—please—that mister stuff . . ." He smiled at Maple. Small and dark, she reminded him of a junco, those little birds that hung out in the pine trees behind his rooming house all winter. Small and quiet, quick and hardy as hell.

"And I'm mighty grateful. This streetcar strike is such an inconvenience. I had to walk nearly three miles in the heat of the day to get here." Maple lived with her grandmother in a modest bungalow on Randolph, the house her mother had been born in.

"I'll just finish my coffee, here, and we can be off," he said, taking a sip.

Maple was done working. Only Conway and three other men sat at the counter, nursing cups of black coffee. The Dot Spot Diner closed at ten. It was now quarter past. Maple loved her job, and worked hard, despite the heat and grease, the lousy tips, the long hours on her feet, and the unwanted attention from some of the older men. She was earning her keep, able to help her grandmother out a bit too. She loved her grandmother, but couldn't help feeling that she was a burden. Maple had been living with her since she was thirteen, when her mother died, her dad having flown the coop years earlier. At nineteen, she felt old enough to take care of herself, but the Depression made it hard going.

Conway's motorcycle stood right outside the door, chrome gleaming, the black saddle smooth and firm. He climbed on first, swinging his leg like an arch over the bike, then settled in. A kick of the pedal and the bike coughed, then purred.

Maple watched. She knew that by sitting on the bike she would be entering his world, and that everyone who saw them would see them together.

Dressed in her work uniform, a white button-down shirt, red polka-dot knee-length skirt, and matching beret with white pompom on top, she was suddenly aware of a problem. How could she ride with Conway, on the back of his bike, and keep her skirt down and her hat on at the same time—with one hand placed casually around his waist?

She swung her leg over the back of the bike, aware of the men in the diner watching her. She settled in next to Conway. Her head came to his shoulders and she felt instantly safe behind this cliff of a man. He backed up and then brought the bike around, down to West Seventh where it moaned, waiting to take off. Somewhere near the Schmidt brewery Maple's hat took flight. It was the first of many things she'd lose with Conway.

~

On November 11, 1941, the temperature dropped so quickly that the chickens on Uncle Hamline's farm flash froze. One of the worst blizzards in the state's history, it caught everyone off guard. The day had been mild and all the hunters and farm animals had been wandering, dazed, in the spring-like weather. From sixty-five degrees to fifteen in a matter of minutes, with the wind and the snow turning everything white, many people were lost until the spring thaw. Pop and Margaret drove out three days later and loaded the trunk with as many chickens as it could hold. When they got home, back to West St. Paul, Pop buried them in the snowbank on the north side of the garage. Every week that winter they ate chicken—after Ma plucked it and cleaned it and drained the blood. A real treat. Fried, baked, with onions, or stuffed with last summer's sage.

~

After getting caught scavenging the caves near the bluffs and stealing mushrooms from Lehman's Cave at the base, Maria, Victoria, and Magnolia were assigned to Laurel—seventeen and boy-crazy. Mama said they could only go to the library or the post office, since Laurel wasn't likely to meet any young men there, and the three younger girls weren't likely to get into too much trouble with the police—Mama making sure to point out the wanted posters at the post office. "Ugly. Every one of those lying cheating scoundrels," Mama always said. "That's why we like good-looking men," she'd say, staring at Laurel. But she was too thick to get it. Anything in pants caught her eye. What Mama didn't know was that on Saturday afternoons Mrs. Jeffers was teaching dance in the basement of the library. Laurel made a big show of how bored she was with the burden of having to take the three delinquents to the library each and every Saturday that summer.

Mrs. Jeffers was a cupcake-shaped woman, chocolate brown and maple-sugar sweet. She kept her afro short and wavy. She loved to dance almost as much as she loved to read. And her eyes made everybody think of stones in a river, smooth and inviting.

When Clarence Miller and his bloodhound Seal were the only males to show that first Saturday (and each one after that despite Mrs. Jeffers's campaign), she folded her arms across her chest and said, "Most men dance like they've got themselves four left feet anyhow." When Seal tucked his tail and tried to slip under a table she proclaimed, "Whichever of you girls can get that dog to dance will be the belle of the ball."

Laurel had him licking her hand before the first song was over, to no one's surprise. Mrs. Jeffers taught the girls how to waltz and schottische, how to boogie and bump. Clarence held each girl's hand like he was dangling twenty feet from the ground by a rope, over an open pit, full of starving wolverines. He tried to make conversation with whichever girl he danced with, but things like "did you know there are eleven misspelled words in the library's copy of *Frankenstein*" came to mind as he danced. Numbers and facts, triangles and trapezoids filled his brain.

Laurel danced with Seal. Maria and Magnolia fought over Victoria, the loser getting Clarence. And Mrs. Jeffers danced with J.D. Salinger, Dickens, or Shakespeare, clutching and swinging and dipping the book as if it were a woman.

Thirty years later, the only dance Clarence remembers is the chicken dance, which is about as useful as the facts about circumference and negative numbers he carries in his head.

~

There was a man by the name of Rockwood who scavenged for beauty and found it in the most unlikely places. A rusted old plow became a trellis, a dead tree was transformed into a cat's paradise when he nailed dainty shelves and tin trays to its limbs, corks from wine bottles were lined up and turned into bulletin boards, shards of broken glass were drilled and hung together to make mosaics and wind chimes.

He was constantly dragging home dead automobiles or the raccoons and cats that running ones killed.

The evening Winthrop and Dale, just boys at the time, helped Rockwood move the claw-footed tub from his neighbor's house to his backyard, Winthrop remembered Dale asking, "Do you think he's crazy? Who'd want to take a bath in their backyard? 'Specially in the winter. I'm not stepping foot in his house. Not with Pa not here."

Their dad worked for the phone company and had been called to check on a down line north of the city, somewhere near Coon Rapids. Dale had wanted to go with him. He loved riding in the truck with his Pa, watching the city turn from buildings and houses to field and sky. Plus he liked the idea of rapids made of coons. But their Pa had said no. Rockwood was an old friend and needed help and Winthrop and Dale could bike over and help him. They lived at Maryland and Prosperity. Riding their bikes past Arcade and Payne Avenues where sin and danger lurked, they turned south on Edgerton winding down the treeless street to Case, then took Mississippi past the junkyards and metal collectors, until they hit Pennsylvania. Sometimes they rode their bikes along the train tracks, hoping the bums and drunks were in town, or too loaded to bother with them. Rockwood's house sat in the neighborhood that bordered the train tracks. Many of the yards grew the same weeds, brambles, and scruffy trees that grew along the tracks.

The tub was too heavy for the three of them to carry, so Rockwood found an old sleigh with runners. He soaped two pieces of cardboard, then wrapped them around the runners. They loaded the tub onto the sleigh (it looked surprisingly similar to the one Santa's team carried through the winter sky) and dragged the tub to his backyard leaving two parallel scars in the neighbor's backyard. Rockwood's yard did not have grass per se. What with the chicken coop (a doghouse with a dollhouse perched on top) and the four dusty chickens it housed, the partial body of an old Chevy truck, and the hood of a Mustang he used as a patio of sorts, the grass didn't have much chance.

The tub was going to stand near the chicken coop, one end buried in the ground. Rockwood had started digging the hole, but had only gotten a few inches down when the boys had arrived, dropping their bikes near the garage along the alley.

The tub and sleigh stopped halfway between the coop and the truck, giving the yard an oval center to the collection of rectangles surrounding it. The four hens meandered around the yard, clucking and cooing, picking here and there in search of something edible.

It was June, and the boys were sweating. Rockwood insisted they come inside and have a glass of lemonade before working on the hole. He knew how much work lay ahead. He didn't have the heart to tell the boys that the diging was hard, but up-ending the tub was going to be even harder. The patio was too hot to sit on—one major drawback to the roof of the Mustang was that it was black metal, and functioned better as a barbecue on long summer nights.

Winthrop caught Dale's eyes. Despite the desire to stay outside, they followed Rockwood into his house. They had never been inside before, had always waited for their Pa on the driveway, or on the stoop.

They sat down at the kitchen table—a large spool that had once held cable wire—on crates that Rockwood had stapled magazines to the top of, and watched as he squeezed lemons and limes, smashed a few strawberries with a can of Campbell's soup, and then stirred it all together. The room was shady and cool, uncluttered and unadorned. Rockwood poured the drink over chunks of ice in jelly jars. Sweet and sour, pink as a girl's blushing cheeks, it was the tastiest thing Winthrop had ever drunk.

It was just about then that Dale asked Rockwood if he was going to bathe in the backyard now, or was the tub going to be a duck pond?

"Bathe in it?" Rockwood laughed, a hearty, from-the-knees-up kind of a laugh. "Oh no," he said. "That old tub's going to house the Virgin Mary. Stand it up, sink it into the ground a couple feet, and then Mary over there can be sheltered from the rain and sun."

Mary was a faded plaster model, standing straight as a board, hands folded, head bent in modest prayer. She wore a pale blue dress and white veil, her hands and face chipped and yellowed.

"Oh," Dale said. Winthrop could tell that his brother thought this was crazier than using the tub to bathe in.

It was then that the chicken Rockwood had named St. Clair wandered in through the dog door, made her way to the table, sat herself down in the middle and laid an egg.

Rockwood picked up the egg, soft and warm, and handed it to Dale.

"Doesn't anything in this place stay where it's supposed to and do what it's supposed to?" Dale considered the egg, then watched as the chicken waddled into the living room, disappearing behind the couch.

Rockwood pursed his lips and tapped his foot slowly. "Why Dale, beauty can be anywhere she wants to be, can't she? You wouldn't expect her to sit in one place. Beauty doesn't work that way. She always surprises you, catches you off guard. Just when you think you've seen everything, there she is making your heart pound or ache."

Winthrop watched as Dale cradled the egg, noticing for the first time how still his younger brother could be, like a portrait. His cheeks rosy from the work, his lips moist and parted, his head bent, his hand as soft and protective as a nest. The egg glowed like a little moon. And for that moment they all believed in beauty, crazy as it seems.

THE INTERVIEW

The Interview

JOANNA RAWSON
West Seventh

[TAPE——SIDE A]

OK. This is June 21, 2002. 0900 hours. West District Station in St. Paul. Detective Frank Gillespie in a first interview with Dennis Hauser.

Det. Frank Gillespie: OK, Dennis. The tape's going. You good in your seat there? You all set? What we're here to do is have you tell what happened yesterday. This is in your own words now, however you want to say it. We're friends, right?

Dennis Hauser: Right. Friends a long time, sir, that is the truth—and I want to not have trouble about this—

FG: I know you don't, Dennis. We're having this little talk to get the trouble settled. OK? We'll take it slow. Let's start with your name.

DH: My name is Dennis James Hauser.

FG: And where do you live?

DH: At 255 Duke Avenue, St. Paul, Minnesota, 55102. In my own house I own myself and have for eighteen years.

FG: And you live alone?

DH: I do live alone, and [. . .] because of it—

FG: Dennis? You need to try hard not to mumble or the tape won't pick up your words. OK? Good. Now, when were you born?

DH: On June 20, in the year 1964.

FG: So your birthday was yesterday, that right?

DH: That is why they came to visit me, yes, that is the reason why—

FG: OK. Let's get to that in a minute. Why don't you begin with yesterday before the trouble.

DH: Can I start at work? I believe that is what I will do—start at work. This is at Hope Middle School where my job is janitor. I go at six in the morning and I work till two, for twenty-one years, three months, ten days as of today, because I like to keep count. It is a year-round school. I am paid and have vacations and am union. This is the school where I went and then Principal McManus hired me to keep it in shape. I got sent there because I am special.

FG: That's right. Because you're special—

DH: Right.

FG: OK. So you were at work yesterday?

DH: Yes, like always. We practiced a tornado drill and then the kids had a picnic and I sat on the steps in the sun watching. I set my gloves and broom on the blacktop and my key ring where it was safe. Mrs. Pritchard brought me a sack lunch and the day was fine so I took it easy, but I was still work-ing and keeping my eyes on where the kids put their garbage, in the can or on the tables, and their toys, in the bin or on the ground, and the mud from their shoes, scraped off or tracked in. I was making a plan for cleaning up.

FG: Which you did.

DH: Yes, I did do my job. I did take care of everything before leaving at three. I put all items where they belonged and all properties in order.

FG: Then what?

DH: I hung my work shirt and changed shoes. Checked the six halls and four bathrooms. Turned off lights. Emptied trash cans. Took down the flag. Secured every lock on doors and windows. I punched out with each matter done on my checklist and left.

FG: Now let me ask you this. What time did you expect your mother and father to arrive for their visit?

DH: My mom said five o'clock or thereabouts on the telephone—to be on the lookout she figured at five since they were coming in from a campground to the south and what about traffic she could not say but just guessed.

FG: Good. So let's pick up from when you left work.

DH: What I do is get on my bike and go around to check on the neighborhood and say hello and how is it going. I know who should be there and who not. I keep an eye on proceedings. Here is a for-instance. There will be time when enough raining and sun means a certain yard needs mowing and so I will do that because I have become aware that the week before the owner of it cracked her hip and can't. Or a time when according to my observations the estranged husband of Juanita on Oneida Avenue cuts through the alley again to spy on his wife and his hair sticks straight up so from behind he looks like a devil and I will call you here at the station and tell. One time she went off to Canada and while she was up there he burned all her panties in a pile in the driveway and I telephoned then too. It might be that Mr. Gaboury's paper stays on the porch till after noon and I will report the reason being I saw him in the hammock at four o'clock the afternoon before on my way by with a lot of beers on the grass and seven already empty so he is now still sleeping and could be sick. What I do is—

FG: Dennis? OK, let's try to stay somewhat focused here—

DH: I am halfway home and just done mowing Helen Maupin's lawn and don't see what good is forcing time any faster. One thing happens and then the next, which is when I get back on my bike—

FG: Right. And you're on your way home—

DH: And I turn down Grace Street going west, like I do on Thursdays. I go by the house of Joe who plays his accordion only on each July the Fourth and then fires his shotgun off the front porch. I do not know where the bullets fall. I go by Humpback's, who caught her couch on fire last winter when her electric valentine shorted out. I turn at the corner of Toronto Street, where I catch the smell from the brewery in the wind, which is sweet from malt but now has the ethanol in it. I did smell it some yesterday, plus Mrs. Wiley's mock orange. What I did was stop at the gate of Barney Lee's and he was on the stoop with his tabby cat perched on his chest who he says likes to listen to the watch in his front pocket. I believe he once shot an elephant with a tranquilizer gun and brought it back to the circus, like a hero. Now he sings "I'll take you home again, Kathleen" to his little cat and makes the little kids next door pee their pants when he looks sideways.

FG: Dennis?

DH: Right, almost there. Now I make my last stop at First City Bank to see the mallards. These are for certain your orderly duck. What they do is come back, every year they come back, and to the same place for the same length and do the same thing. In the third week of April they arrive like always. They nest and hatch babies they raise to fly who then do fly. They get done with that work and next year do that work again. I saw them do it first when the place was a marsh lake that filled with runoff and early rain and the weeds they like for hiding. We called it Bottom's Pond back then. It would turn black with mosquitoes in summer. I found a man's false leg in the shallows there once that belonged to a Mr. Orville who survived his ship being bombed and sunk in the war. Then they drained that pond out and paved it and built the bank on it but the ducks still come back. They don't know better. I believe it is habit. They go right under the tangle of shrubs off the blacktop by the drive-up cash machine and do what they do and I check on them each day and did yesterday.

FG: And that was your last stop?

DH: It was, last on my rounds—4:37 by the clock on my bike. I expected company and meant to be sure all things were set and at the door for them driving up.

FG: Now Dennis, would you say for the record who it was you were expecting?

DH: That would be my mom and my dad, coming in because of my birthday, which they did after finding me again after my getting lost.

FG: Is it right that their names are Delores May Hauser and Clarence Ides Hauser?

DH: That is right even if my mom likes to go by Dolly instead because otherwise she says she sounds fat.

FG: Now explain what you mean by "getting lost."

DH: By that I will repeat what she tells me, which is that I got lost at the children's hospital in downtown St. Paul in 1968 when I was four with pneumonia and my mom took me there to the wet room to mend awhile and doctors moved me to a different room because I was so special and did not bother to inform her where and she could not find me for all these years as if I had been stolen. They finally got news of my whereabouts from the official agency that handles such losses and came. She says divine intervention, that is the truth. I had stayed with some families here and there and that was fine while waiting because she would be sick with grief, as I remember she would say when I was little that it made her sick, sick with grief to think how special I was. They were to come this year in their car and stay just overnight because they are busy people going from a snowbird camp to Canada for the summer—

FG: Real migrants, huh? What is it your mother and father do for money, Dennis?

DH: My dad is a man who has some concerns, sir, and I am told my mom manages these. They also work some for the government and draw a check for that. She says it is not beyond them to afford a spree, as on my birthday, which they were already there for when I rode up yesterday.

FG: Were they inside at that time?

DH: No, sir, at the car. I have the one house key on my ring so they were parked at the curb and under the hood tinkering with the radio on. My neighbor Shirley was there telling what she tells to whoever listens, which is about the time she was sitting on the front bumper of her best friend's 1955 baby blue Chevrolet and it slipped into neutral and her sweater caught and she got dragged two blocks downhill and all her skin wore off and the priest read last rites six times before she stayed alive. I shook my dad's hand and my mom's too, because of her cold she would not want to pass to me, and we went inside to cool off and eat the supper I put together at the table set for three, but then my mom said, Let's go out, we've been on the road all day so let's go out to eat and my dad says yes.

FG: So it was their idea to leave, that right?

DH: It was, since I myself had earlier laid new plates and a center arrangement and had a menu fixed. The mistake I made was in not asking before about what they would want, in or out, and so I put it away and we went thinking just McDonald's and then why not a bit fancier, which was Mancini's. We walked over there—

FG: Hold on—did you lock the house up when you left?

DH: Let me tell you I do that always. I have had trouble before. I have changed the locks before. I have the one key—I keep it here on my belt. I use it to lock up and did that last night. My house was locked tight. Yes, sir. It was. I did—

FG: OK, Dennis. Simple question. No need to get worked up. Front light on?

DH: Yes.

FG: OK. So you had the dinner out.

DH: The host did not make us wait since I mow the grass there and do the flowers. Specials were on the board, a fish and a T-bone, and my dad says, Shit, no cheap chops, and I got to feeling bad for that and wanted him to stay in the good mood he came in so said, Whatever you want you order, just order and have, and my mom says, Honey, Dennis is right and it's his birthday and he'll pay for what you want because it's a party. So he did order that and my mom too, with some cocktails, then the waitress brought a little sundae and candle and we sang.

FG: What happened then?

DH: Well, at the time it gets dark now, which depends and changes—

[TAPE—SIDE B. June 21, 2002, Detective Frank Gillespie and Dennis Hauser]

DH: —yesterday that would have been around 9:20 but still light enough to walk back through the park. They were laughing and my mom says, Dennis, sometimes I just break into gladness that you turned out so good, and she laughed more and did what she called her coffin cough and said, Give over another smoke, Clarence, and then, did I remember her from before? We were at the playground and she shooed some youngsters off the swings and got on one and said to push her, which I did do. She said, Do you remember and if you do, exactly what?

I told her no, no I could not remember a thing except the hospital where I got lost when I was so little, just that the air was like steam and the machine by my bed sounded sometimes like wind and sometimes like a cricket was stuck in it. That's all. She was very high then and said, Dennis, go under, go under and push me, so I caught her legs and yanked all the way and she almost popped out but was still laughing until she threw up on the grass and we quit.

After that we stretched on the field very quiet and just breathing under the stars, with them all arranged right and my mom humming as I remember she once did. My dad started to snore and then she whispered real low, Dennis, you are still a very special boy. It was not for me to say a thing back

but just to lie there and be still. I heard planes going over and a dog close by.
I studied the fireflies swarmed up along the tracks and making me think of
candles on a thousand-year-old birthday cake. I watched the end of her cigarette in her shaky hand going up and down and scribbling in the dark till
she said let's go.

Shirley was out watering her prize roses when we came by. I unlocked and
we went in and when I was busy putting my leftovers from supper in the
fridge I heard my dad crack a window and my mom go in the bedroom still
humming. I would say that is when this trouble started up—

FG: ok. Now let's take this next part slow. What's the next thing you remember?

DH: Next thing is my mom comes running from the bedroom screeching,
Dennis, Dennis, somebody stole all my money! Somebody came in here
and filched it all! She let out a noise and waved around this little yellow
bag and shrieked more and I caught her by the arm and she sort of fell
sideways and pulled me with my dad up and right behind us into the bedroom and yells, He came in here and found my stash! Yells, All my five
hundred dollars is disappeared, it's ripped off. Do something! Somebody
do something! Which she kept barking and flinging things from her suitcase and then cries, Dennis, oh—how could you let him come in here?
Somebody—oh—

FG: Hold on—what was your father doing?

DH: Standing there, and did not say any word but look how upset your
mother is and then put his hand upon my shoulder with a pinch. She hung
down her head and yanked her hair. She muttered how this is bad, I knew
this was a bad idea to come, why'd we come here? Then he tells me to think
over what I had better do and says, Dolly, I'll be on the stoop.

FG: Did you see any signs of disturbance?

DH: Just Mom. Just her disturbance. If you mean broken items or some riffling through, I did not see that, no sir, that is the truth. I am known to keep a neat house for the sake of keeping track of things and thrift. There are shelves, there are drawers and closets, plus pillows where they belong and a place for papers. I believe a blind man in my house could get along fine. Were a thing fiddled with I could tell right away. I will say from then till now I have been stumped how the thief came to be inside but do recognize some limitations from my being special and so after going over it, screens and door mechanisms and the padlocked cellar and dryer chute and chimney stack and even on a spur thought the basement sewer pipe that hooks to the main, I can come to no answer. Oh, this robber he is a sly one who is making it his business to trick me and to steal the bottom dollar from my mom in the off-guard hours—but how is beyond me.

FG: That's what we're here to find out, Dennis. It might've been better all around if you'd called down to the station here last night and reported it. But you didn't do that, did you?

DH: No, I did not do it.

FG: Because?

DH: Well, it did not seem best to—

FG: Is that what you thought at the time? Or is that—

DH: What I thought, yes, it was my thinking on that after I said to her, Why not call my police friend Frank Gillespie and he will make a plan of capture and get your money, which will solve this trouble while there is the chance of him lurking in the neighborhood. But no. No don't, she said, and was getting upset once more and her voice rising. I said, All right, and she said, No, it is not, my cash is filched from your house. She said, Go find the thief and get it back, I know you can, Dennis, and then we'll be safe to come for your birthday next year. You know what to do, son, she said.

So I answered to lock the door behind me and wheeled my bike out in the dark and put on my orange vest for night travel and my two lights, the front and the back, checked the tires and the spare and the fix kit and horn, like always. I looked at the front window and saw the blue light from the TV and my dad inside with her on the couch watching. I started the lookout for this prowler not knowing how he appeared, but figured in black and a cap, like a thief does, in a shadow or bush or heading for escape by way of the tracks, so I turned on Palace Avenue and rode around for 2.8 miles by my odometer and through each street and checked the clock mounted on the handlebars that helps me organize time when I am out. I saw it was 12:13 in the morning and quiet each place I tried. After a while I could not think of any others without going into unknown parts, which I did not want to do alone with the moon from earlier clouded over. I came around to Fort Road where in the past when I have had a disturbed sleep I would travel to wear the nerves down and see third shifts of workers from the Ford plant on the river heading home, but I did not see that traffic. I talked to myself like this—said, Dennis, you will not find this thief tonight. He is a clever being and camouflaged into a blind spot now. It will take some daylight and take help. You have not one or the other at this time.

FG: Is that when you decided to give up?

DH: Oh, no, sir—I did not give up. It was then I thought it best to make a stop of the search but only temporary. My method for streets and places was thrown off. So the reasoning this tracking needed was shot and better to start new in the morning against the slyness of him. Also my mom. She may have fallen apart from worry by then. What sort of bad neighborhood I live in and unsafe house and invaders stealing around and into it, well, she would conclude, which I did not want. I have a good place. I am careful. I take care of things and would not want a person thinking otherwise. At that time I thought to just go over to the bank a block away and the cash machine there and take out the money to cover her loss so she would cheer up—then in the morning take up the search and find the thief and get her five hundred right into the bank again like nothing ever happened.

Which I did do, being as I keep my balance over the minimum for interest-free and so had it. I got that no-small-amount and put the receipt in my pocket, which I have brought today as proof of burglary and my solving it as far as concerns my mom until the culprit is brought in. Next I wheeled up the curb and back toward where the mallards are in that thicket for shelter. I could not see a single thing but knew what was there. I made little noise so as to not disturb—could be they were sleeping in peace.

The truth is that my house being dark was not a surprise. They were in bed and every light off. I cracked that door and no one stirred so I tiptoed in and wondered what next while just listening to their breathing until I could make out her suitcase on the chair. That is where I put the money, right in the little yellow bag. Then just neatened up—folded her blouse that was in a twist on the floor and also her soiled things. I wanted to not wake her up but did a moment because her eyes opened when I looked over. She whispered words I could not hear so I moved closer and kneeled there and she said, Did you catch him, honey? Did you get my money? I said to her, Yes, yes Mom, I did do that.

FG: You told her you caught the thief?

DH: Yes, I did do that.

FG: And that was a lie?

DH: It was a lie I told, which is not my usual way of doing things. I did hope that her knowing it would be a comfort and I believe it was, because she patted my arm then and whispered, Good.

FG: Dennis, if we need your mom and dad to come down to the station and corroborate this information—

DH: Oh, it would be a hard thing. I got up this morning and they were packed and gone. She left a note to say sorry for not staying on for the breakfast I had planned.

FG: I see. Now, Dennis, listen—can you recall what make and model their car was, and the license plate?

DH: It was a station wagon with the panels, blue and brown with some rust and crumpling on the left side, not so new and with items strapped up top—a campstove and lawn chairs and maybe a birdcage and one spare tire. The license I could not say. It was a different automobile than the one driven last year and it—

FG: Last year? Do you mean they were here last year?

DH: Yes, sir, for my birthday, on their first visit. At the very same time I got my house broken into last year and my mom had her money stolen then too. After that trouble I replaced the locks and buttoned the windows and cellar up.

FG: Why didn't you report this to us?

DH: Oh, my mom did not want to do that because it would shame her and why have police think I could not protect my visitors from this intruder.

This morning I did think to not call authorities until Principal McManus at the school, on seeing I was somewhat down and tired, asked what was the matter. This was her idea to come right down.

FG: OK—I think we've got enough to go on. Now I want you to take a minute and think, think real hard about this, Dennis. If this should end up with a prosecution, in court, say, and we need you to come back in and testify, would you do that?

DH: I would not mind doing that except I do not want my neighbors to be afraid of this sort of trouble. I believe when you do locate this swift thief and find the five hundred of this year and that of last year and put him in jail then yes, I will say what it is he did to us. That is the truth.

[END TAPE]

THE CATCHER

The Catcher

NORA MURPHY

Lexington Outreach

On Memorial Day the St. Peter Clavier Choir belts out songs like "Gracious Redeemer" and "Amazing Grace" with Manny Markham's voice leading them down into the lower scales and back up far beyond middle c. To crescendo and close the songs, they would look to Manny for his hand signals—left over from his days as a catcher.

But on this Memorial Day, no one knew where Manny was.

The sopranos couldn't find him in the small clouds that drifted across the early summer sky. The altos didn't hear him echo in the cottonwood leaves. The baritones didn't spy him hiding between the stone markers that spread across the lawn like eighth notes in a piece by Gershwin. The basses couldn't hear his voice tremble when they sent their beat into the earth below.

Kate Markham didn't know where her father-in-law was either. She was the mother of his twin grandchildren. The Memorial Day service at Calvary Cemetery was a Markham family tradition. But their attendance this year was spotty—just Kate and the twins. The rest of the Markhams were up at the house on Dayton Avenue waiting to see who would show up first—Manny or the police.

Kate was white. She had married Manny's son George in 1960 when they were students at the University of Minnesota. Neither family had welcomed the marriage, but when Kate got pregnant with the twins, the Markham's parish, St. Peter Clavier, had agreed to marry them. Kate's family parish had not.

The choir's dissipated version of "Holy Father, Holy Son" was the least of Kate Markham's troubles this morning. Seven-year-old Paul had been sitting at the base of the cottonwood tree behind the celebrants ten minutes ago. Now he was gone.

The other twin, Troy, sat cross-legged in the grass, smiling. He rocked back and forth to the music—finding the beat that the singers had lost that morning. Troy didn't miss Grandpa Markham.

But Paul did.

He thought he could find him, too. Paul had heard his grandfather's voice humming from the other side of the cemetery. It was warm, like the morning sun on Paul's freckled face. So without even glancing back at his mother or Troy, Paul headed east past the cottonwood tree and out of the cemetery. When he reached the railroad tracks, the humming dimmed.

Paul didn't know which way to turn—to the left where he could see the big "1" on top of the bank downtown, or toward the empty sky on his right. He paused, remembering something Grandpa Markham had told him a few weeks earlier.

"You must remember that twins are blessed," his grandfather had said when Paul felt neglected because his mom and grandmother were fussing over a small knee scrape that Troy had gotten in the alley.

Paul leaned into his grandfather. They had identical faces—only their size and color distinguished them. Grandpa Markham's skin was dark like the night sky when the first star comes out. Paul's was light and creamy like the eggs that Aunt Candy brought every weekend from the farm stand near her house.

"The Yoruba people say that everyone is born with a sky double—a celestial twin. The twin in the sky is like a god. When the sky double makes a move in heaven, their twin on earth mirrors it. They say that when twins are both born on earth, the sky double got put here for some special reason. But no one—not even their mother—knows which of the twins is the sky twin. So everyone must treat both twins with great respect."

Looking into his eyes to see if he was joking, Paul felt his grandfather's belly jiggle with laughter. "Oh, it's probably just a story, son, but you never know. Maybe Troy is your sky double and that's why he gets a lot of attention—even for a scraped knee. In the meanwhile, be careful what you say and think about your brother."

Paul didn't understand how either he or Troy could be gods, but the story comforted him today. He decided to turn away from the buildings downtown and head right toward the open sky along the railroad tracks.

Kate smiled with Troy and trusted that Paul would reappear from the other side of the cottonwood when the service was over. She turned her thoughts to the Mass. She followed the priest and the prayers, as well as her own thoughts.

The phone call announcing Manny Markham's disappearance came before the twins had woken up. George hopped into the shower and pleaded, "Kate, you'll be fine with the boys at the Memorial Day service, won't you? Someone needs to represent the Markhams there. I need to be at home to keep my mother company."

The first time Kate met Elizabeth Farrington Markham, George had brought her home for Sunday dinner. While George and his father talked about the upcoming game between the St. Paul Saints and the Minneapolis Millers at one end of the table, Mrs. Markham cornered Kate at the other. George's sister Candy tried to referee.

Kate remembered faltering at every one of Mrs. Markham's questions. She remembered Candy's sympathetic eyes. Kate learned that her father and Mrs. Markham's father had been attorneys on opposite sides of a legal case. Ryan v. The St. Paul Hotel. Mr. Hazel, a black man, had taken The St. Paul Hotel to court for refusing him entry there. At first, no one wanted to represent Mr. Hazel. Mrs. Markham's father had taken it on—it was one of his last cases. Kate's father, who was just starting his legal career, had represented The St. Paul Hotel. Mr. Hazel won. Kate wasn't so sure her father would like knowing that she was going to marry Mrs. Markham's son.

But she had married George and here she was now—the only adult representative of the Markham family at the St. Peter Clavier Memorial Day Service. The service came to a close as the sun passed the midpoint of the eastern sky. Everyone—choir members, altar boys, and celebrants—started weaving in and around the grave markers carrying things that had to get back to the church. Kate helped load missals, candles, and folding chairs into the parish wagon. Then she watched Troy belt himself into the backseat of their 1967 Falcon station wagon.

Kate realized then that Paul had not returned.

She drove the station wagon at top speed to the senior Markham's house, lurched to a stop, and ran out, leaving Troy in the backseat.

"George . . . George," she called, as she pushed open the front screen door and ran back to the kitchen where George, Candy, and their mother sat, waiting by the telephone.

"It's Paul. I can't find him. He's gone," she cried.

"Slow down now," George soothed. Then he turned to Candy and asked her to check on Troy.

After the police left—for the second time that day—the Markhams waited for the two family members who had gone AWOL. Nobody felt like cooking, or even slicing up the leftover chicken for sandwiches on Elizabeth Markham's fresh bread. Nobody felt like talking. Instead they listened to the sounds in the back of the house.

George tapped his fingers in time to the grandfather clock in the dining room. The coffee pot on the stove gurgled as Candy heated a cup for Kate. House sparrows sang outside the back door. No one dared look at the phone or at Mrs. Markham—fearful that they might jinx them.

Troy eventually spoke up. He was hungry. "I want a Dreamsicle."

"A Dreamsicle, son?" George asked, reaching out to rub his quiet son's shoulders.

"A Dreamsicle, Daddy. The kind that is orange and soft and like a cloud when you bit it."

"Well, I suppose we could find you one," responded George. "Kate, I'll run up to the Red Owl with Troy."

Half a mile down the tracks Paul could finally hear his grandfather's hum again. He followed it south, toward University Avenue and the new freeway. As he walked, Paul remembered playing catch with his grandfather after church last Sunday. Grandpa Markham had thrown the ball so high it almost touched the sky.

"Tell me about being a catcher," Paul said, tossing his grandfather the ball.

When Grandpa Markham threw the ball back to Paul, he missed it. Grandpa had teased him, "Eyes on the ball, now. Being a catcher isn't as easy as you might think, son. Catching the ball is the least of our worries. You have to know the way every player bats, you have to have the eye of every team member on you, you have to think fast and throw even faster. If you've got a good catcher, it means you've got a good team. Every team in the Negro Baseball Leagues feared going up against the Black Barons—because not a single team could break our codes, and no other catcher could throw or think as fast as your grandfather."

Paul threw the ball back to his grandfather and watched him pluck it out of the air and make the ball disappear in his glove like magic. Then he sat down on the picnic bench to listen.

"Back in the days, Paul, back in the days when I first came to St. Paul on the circuit and met your grandmother. We weren't allowed to stay in the same hotels as white folks, so we'd get invited to the homes of families in the community."

Manny took a seat next to his grandson and continued. "We played at the Lexington Baseball Field in St. Paul. Everyone paid to watch the Black

Barons play. But at night, when the games were over, we'd shuttle over to Erma Wilson's big house on Rondo Avenue.

"Mrs. Wilson's house was one of the best places to stay when you were on the road. She had pitchers of cool lemonade and punch that never went empty. She knew how to cook, too.

"After dinner, we'd get ready for her famous parties. We'd push back the table and chairs to reveal Erma Wilson's smooth polished floors. She'd turn on her phonograph and play the records of all the black singers who had stayed at her house—like Ella Fitzgerald. The whole neighborhood showed up and we'd dance until dawn."

"Isn't that where Grandma twisted your arm?" asked Paul, squinting into his grandfather's bright eyes.

Grandpa Markham laughed, "In fact, that's the year my arm got twisted two times. First off, I hurt my arm in a game against the Homestead Grays. You know, they had a fine catcher, too. A young man from Philadelphia named Roy Campanella. Unlike me, that Campy could hit, too. He proved it in a game on a night that I'll never forget. It was the bottom of the fourth inning, Campy was up to bat and I called for a fastball—like this . . ."

He stood up and squatted into position, showing Paul the secret hand signal he'd used almost thirty years before.

"The Grays were already ahead by two runs. But that wasn't the worst of our troubles. For the first time in the history of the Black Barons, someone broke our code. Campy was ready for the fastball. He hit to right field. The ball grazed Harrison's outstretched glove and ricocheted off the back fence into the foul ball corner. By the time Harrison reached the ball, Campy was rounding second. When Harrison had thrown the ball to the cutoff man, Campy had just passed third.

"As he slid toward home, I had to jump up to catch the ball. When I came down, I was more than a foot away from the plate. I leaned in, fell, and ended up breaking my arm. Campy scored, the Grays won, and I was out for the rest of the season."

Manny Markham stood up and tossed the ball back to Paul.

"Good catch, Son. Well, I knew then that baseball wasn't going to carry me through life. I didn't have hurt feelings about it. So I even rooted for Campy the year he played for the St. Paul Saints—your father remembers meeting him in 1947. You see, the night of my accident was the night that I met the true love of my life."

"That night, a group of young ladies, escorted by their older brothers and cousins, arrived for the dance at Erma Wilson's. Your grandmother was one of them. We all knew who her father was—the lawyer who won a famous case that let a black man stay at The St. Paul Hotel. So I figured she'd be smart, but until Mrs. Wilson introduced us that night, I never expected her to be so beautiful. Her beauty hit me faster than any pitcher's fastball ever had. It still does."

The first thing Paul noticed when he crossed University Avenue was the Red Owl grocery store. The sadness inside him sounded louder than Grandpa Markham's voice. His feet hurt, he missed his parents, and he wondered if Troy was OK. Paul sat down on a concrete divide in the parking lot and stared at the painted red owl that loomed over the lot. Tears drifted slowly down his face. He was too tired to wipe them away.

"How about a Dreamsicle, son?"

Paul looked up. A familiar voice in a familiar car pulled up beside him. It was his father.

"Hi Paul!" waved Troy, leaning out of the window in the backseat. "We're getting Dreamsicles. Want one?"

George parked the car and walked around to hug Paul. "Long day, son? Your mother is worried sick about you. Come on in. I bet you're hot. A little ice cream will do you good."

They walked into the Red Owl, shivering in the air conditioning. Troy led the way to the back of the store. George and Paul followed, holding hands. In that grasp, Paul's tears flowed more than ever. He didn't want his father to see him cry, but he wanted to let go even less.

"Here they are, here they are," shouted Troy.

George opened the freezer case and pulled out the orange and blue box of ice cream treats. As he closed the case, he saw someone he hadn't expected to see reflected in the silver handle.

Manny Markham stood staring at the ground in the meat section around the corner.

George hushed the twins and walked toward his father.

"Father?" George asked softly.

Manny didn't answer. He pointed with his feet to the bronze plaque set into the grocery store floor.

"Home plate for the old Lexington Ball Field," said George. "Your plate."

Manny still didn't say anything.

"Let's go home now. Mama misses her catcher."

THE FAT-BRUSH
PAINTER

The Fat-Brush Painter

DIEGO VÁZQUEZ, JR.
Skyway

The murder took place downstairs from my apartment on Prior Avenue North. This is the first time I have lived anywhere close to the "nice" parts of St. Paul, just a few blocks away from Summit Avenue. I just moved into the building the day before yesterday; today I was questioned by the cops. I heard nothing. I saw nothing. I know that my downstairs neighbor was a pretty blonde from Floodwood, Minnesota and that she played Tejano music loudly during the afternoon. In two days prior to the alleged murder the only thing I noticed was loud music playing between the hours of 3:30 and 5:00 P.M. If she had not met her sad destiny, I was going to ask her to play some requests.

The apartment downstairs was sealed in yellow tape and the window shades were shut. The rumor was that the killing resulted from a love triangle. The newspaper reported that witnesses saw two men drive up and that the passenger entered the apartment while the driver waited in the car. The Minneapolis paper would not say what color the suspects were, but the St. Paul paper said that it appeared to have been an Asian driver and a white passenger, and that the killer ran outside in a frenzy but the car did not immediately speed away. The police thought it odd that the car drove away so slowly. The two suspects were still at large.

I miss the music. And I wanted the new vacancy to turn into a job.

I work as a painter in St. Paul. I am known as the Fat-Brush Painter. Through the years I have become well-known both for my artistry and for my grumpiness. I no longer paint houses in Minneapolis. This intrigues many of my St. Paul clients. A few have even commented that they hired me for a particular job because they had heard of my painting ban on Minneapolis houses. I have recently been doing quite a lot of work on the remodeling of the St. Paul downtown Central Library.

There is a long trail of bad dreams and broken bottles and scattered pieces of my heart on the road to my having landed this wonderful job. Let me tell you how a painter like me gets to paint inside this temple of books.

Let me tell you what it has taken me a lifetime to know about painting. Start young with no direction in your life. Find a part-time job in the summer. Work for any number of oddball thieves, liars, ex-cons, and soon-to-be corporate execs, but only work for the guys who will treat you right. Early on you'll learn not to take shit from anybody. Your boss has all the right in the world to tell you what to do on the job, but he cannot tell you what to do about your soul. Early on I was big on learning about my soul.

I am now the best painter in the world. It was a spectacular decision for me to only take on paint jobs for people that I like. I *must* like them. It's very simple. The final question my soul asks my heart is "would these people ever hurt a living thing deliberately?" Spiders count, but their webs don't. I must clear the webs for the paint job to be done properly. Wasps don't count, just because I don't like the hurts that they put on me. And all of their nests must be pushed off the eaves. And if I have to work in a cold, scary basement there better not be any critters in the dark waiting to bite me. They will become the color I am painting.

This spring I hired an assistant, like I do almost every spring, to help out over the busy summer season. I always hire either high school or college kids. But none are ever going to be as well-known as the most recent kid. Orlando Vang. Yeah, I know Hmong names do not include Orlando. Orlando was the first one to give me this piece of information. He also told me that his real first name only had consonants and that I should forget about asking him for it because there was no way in hell that I would get to the tonal place where I could pronounce it right. I liked him immediately.

Then I added my painter's wisdom to the conversation. "So, Orlando. Who gave you the name? Were your parents trying to give one up for America or what?"

Orlando Vang gave me a look like he was from Texas. It was a look Mexican cowboys give each other when they hear Anglos talking about cowboys only being from the United States. Then he drawled like a Tex-Mex singer, "Well, no. My parents did not give me the name. I just took it last year and most of my family is still in shock. Some of them even have started to call me Orlando, but for the most part when I am at home I am still all of those consonants with the special tone."

I stood in silence and recognition. I have always felt an affinity for rebellion. "Oh," I said.

Orlando continued, "Do you know that Total gas station on Seventh before you head out to the airport? The one across from Taco Bell and that tittie bar that has a name that I can never remember? A bunch of years ago, when I was about five or six . . ."

I interrupted the young Vang. "A bunch of years ago. Shit, man, that was like last year for you. For me that would truly be a bunch of years. I wish I could remember being five or six. Yeah, sorry. Go on."

"Why all you old timers always got to get all goofy with your memory? Man, get over it. You guys just old and too bad! And don't forget you get uglier too!"

"Thanks, spring chicken."

"Well, so when I was about five or six, no, I was still five. Anyway, at that time my older cousin Lou Vang, well, 'Lou' is the closest to American that we got with his real name. Lou was nineteen. He told me a story about when he was five years old and when he first came to America. He wanted me to hear it because he said then I would always understand his heart. He said we had the same eyes for the world and that maybe someday we would both be kings in America. He meant kings of our own destiny.

"The sponsors who brought his family over here were from Orlando, Florida. And for my cousin Lou the very first thing he remembers about being in America is living in a town called Orlando and having been taken to a magic kingdom. He thought that the entire America was going to be exactly like Disney World. All he remembers is that for his first few weeks in this country he was inside the Magic Kingdom almost daily. I don't remember the details about why he got to go there so often. Something to do with the church people who were his sponsors also had great connections with the Disney empire. And when cousin Lou started going to school he learned that Orlando can be a person's name. He told his parents that he wanted to change his name to Orlando, that when he becomes king of his destiny he wants to be known as the great king Orlando. His parents ignored him and did not change his name. I wish they could have changed his destiny.

"Lou at nineteen had become a thug, a young criminal who sought glory and pride within a gang that he wanted to lead. Lou and four other young thugs walked into that Total on a bright sunny day for cigarettes and candy and executed three people. They shot the clerks and one customer simply because they wanted to become murderous thugs. They killed three innocent people and to this day my cousin does not have an answer for me. He was put away for life because Minnesota does not have the death penalty. I am probably the only member in my family that stays in touch with him. Last year I sent him a letter that explained to him that I wanted to honor the good part of his life and that I was changing my name to Orlando because I believe to this day that if he could have followed his dream and changed his name then he would not be where he is right now. I want to make certain that I become the king of my destiny and so now I am Orlando. I am another creation for the good from the Magic Kingdom."

It was the first time I ever had to put my brush down while talking and painting. I am expert with the brush, skinny or fat. But I had to stop and stare and look deep into the paint can. I would not tear up. I would do that later alone at home with a beer and the Twins on television. I would remember that my real name is Jimmy Enriquez. That long before I became the "Fat-Brush" I was simply Texas Jimmy. Long ago I too had a cousin who got sour on the fine side of life and got gunned down without his shoes, wearing only his white boxers, while scrambling outside his shack to get the morning paper. The most important details are that the shots came from the underbelly of the kingdom and that I have never owned a gun. I had to learn to shoot and use weapons while in the Army but that does not count.

"Sorry to hear about your cousin, kid. It must be tough on the entire family. Especially since he was the bad guy."

Orlando and I entered a self-imposed silence and in the distant sky the rumble of thunder announced that we would have a short day of outside painting.

Ten years ago, after my divorce, I told myself that I would forevermore only paint when the potential for the job felt good. This meant that it would be difficult to work on crews such as Lamar's because painting was simply business for most painters. I got my start in this city with old Lamar. But after my divorce I had to become more than just a painter. I had to become a painter with a soul. I still bid on any jobs that were available but if the people I would be spending the next few weeks with were not likable to me, I refused to take the job. This was a crazy attitude in the beginning, but after a while I got to like it more and more. I am not that picky. I get along with the world. I am peaceful. I am mostly just a speck of dust. Not a great leader, not a great follower, not a believer in any religion that comes between me and God. This eliminates all known religions, so that God and I are pretty much alone out here.

The message from Lamar was frantic. "Jimmy. Wake up, you lazy painter. I bet it is only two in the morning. Here is the deal. I need some help for two, maybe three days this week. This is a job I am squeezing in, but if things work out, hell, you can take the rest of the project for yourself. It could be a year of work. I think you will like this building. It is the renovation of the St. Paul Central Library. They forgot to include the bathrooms and the hallways and some other out-of-the-way walls when the original bid was awarded to Fresh Coat crew. So I got this little emergency side deal with them. And the money is good. By the way, I still can't believe you turned down that Viking football player's house. Just because the son of a bitch is a spoiled brat athlete with a gorgeous wife, hell, you would have seen more of her than him. Anyway, call me, and let's meet at you-know-where."

I think every important business deal that Lamar ever conducted took place at Arnellia's around six. When I walked in the door he started fast and black, "You know, Texas J, I was starting to give up on you. I still can't believe you walked away from that Vikings job. They were going to pay you top dollar. And how do you know he beats the wife? And how do you know he fools around on her? And how do you know what they do in private? You think the worst, well you get the worst. Besides, they weren't paying you for family counseling, they were paying you to paint the goddamn house. Oh, Texas Jimmy the Tease. How have you made it this far?"

I laughed with him. "Yeah, well this painter is still un cero a la izquierda sin huevos."

Lamar grunted, "ok, what did you just say? And stop pretending like you can still speak Spanish. I only hear you swear in your old tongue. I've never heard you talk to a woman in Spanish."

"I said that this painter is a zero to the left with no balls. Yeah, I am losing my old language. I wonder what it would be like to make love in Spanish again. It's been so long I forget what it sounds like."

Lamar is a historian. "A loser like you and you can't remember doing it in Spanish?"

Lamar insisted that the library job would last at least a year. "There is so goddamn much touch-up that was not in the contract that you will be living under stairways and sleeping in bathrooms while painting your fatbrush heart out." Lamar and I worked out the details because he was simply getting a long-term finders fee for me. His crews were too stretched out and besides, he and I were still friends. At times he would remind me that he was probably the only friend I had, and often times I did not want to admit that he was right.

I told Orlando Vang that when he finished his summer Artswork apprentice program that I could still use his help as much as possible. I also let him know that if all worked out during the coming school year that I could give him quite a lot of after school and weekend work. Orlando was nervous and answered with a sense of urgency. "I will work as much as you want, boss. I just hope I can be around to help. Off the books or on the books. Just let me know and believe me I will keep you out of trouble. If you want to do a cash deal with me I won't let anyone know. Either way. I am here. But I think some trouble is coming my way."

"Orlando, I think I better keep everything straight on the library project. And it doesn't make any difference for you, it is my ass that gets in trouble. But what do you mean that some trouble is coming your way? What did you do? Were you late for a class or something? I know. You were late with a library book. I just can't imagine you in any sort of big trouble. We will just paint away on weeknights and weekends when there are no other painters in the building. There is a goofy arrangement with Lamar that his crew cannot do any work there while Fresh Coat is working. Good thing for us that that crew is all eight-to-five. Hell, if I was the lead crew I would have my guys working from six to three. I love those hours.

"Hey kid, by the way, where you going to college next year?" We were both underneath a stairway at the library on a Saturday morning in November.

Orlando stopped painting in order to expound. "Well, Texas Jimmy, if I don't get sent to prison I am going to attend a school that I bet you have never heard of. I won't take your money, though, because I *know* you have never heard of it. Nobody has heard of it." He resumed painting and continued to talk nervously. My parents want me to go to either Stanford or Harvard. Both schools have already accepted me, but I am not going to either one. Those schools would be too damn boring for me. I need the magnificent stimulation that something like painting walls does for me. I just cannot imagine any course offered at either school that could give me the knowledge that I have gotten from working with you these past few months. Damn, Texas, I think I'll start calling you *Professor Texas*. But I might need a lawyer pretty soon."

"Hey Orlando. What's up? Why do you keep talking about being in trouble? Something happened, eh? You didn't get her in trouble, did you? I thought you didn't have a girlfriend. You ready to talk about it? And no way I want to be called professor anything. I am not a teacher, goddamnit. I am not a follower. . . ."

Orlando interrupted my litany, "Yeah, yeah. I have heard it a thousand times, 'I am not a teacher. I am not a follower. I am not a leader. Although I do want to be a benevolent despot for my selected harem.'"

I told him that I lived in Orlando for a short time before I went on a clandestine venture with the *Venceremos Brigade* to Cuba. I also told him the story of my first visit to the not-yet-opened Disney World. Orlando listened intently to each detail, this being the first story of mine that the young Vang had visibly paid attention to. He mumbled a wish to go there someday.

"So, *Orlando*, you've never been to *Orlando* and the Magic Kingdom?"

"No. And what was the *Venceremos Brigade?*"

"It was a leftist radical bunch who secretly went to Cuba to help with the sugarcane harvest during the late part of the sixties. I never really went with them to Cuba; it is such a long-ass story. The short version is that I was trying to get laid and this gorgeous woman that had me by los huevos made me chase her all over the country. I ended up in Orlando because a bunch of these radical cane pickers were working on the opening of Disney World. They were damn good with their fronts. Anyway, her connection to Disney was through theater. She did stuff with the original Disneyland in Anaheim. 'Trained a bunch of Mickeys and Minnies how to act Goofy,' she would say. And they had sent her as a consultant for the opening of the new Magic Kingdom. She was there waiting for the signal to leave for Canada. Complicated, huh? These guys had to board ships in Canada in order to get to Cuba. Well, Orlando is as far as I went with her. Once her secret signal came to leave I followed my chicken-ass heart and said good-bye. I just could not cross that line and she left me without my ever getting to be her lover. Damn, I still think I should have gone with her. Here I am painting walls and she teaches American Government courses at Berserkly . . . Berkeley."

Orlando listened and laughed and continued to paint. "So, what is the Magic Kingdom like? I hope I get a chance to see it."

I noticed that Orlando was nervous but I continued talking. "The first time I went it was twenty-six degrees. I was there during a hundred-year record cold spell. It was disastrous for all of the oranges and was very memorable at Disney World. The place was not yet fully opened and I got to go in during a run-through . . . where everyone practices for the opening. Man, all I remember is my teeth chattering. No one was prepared for that cold day. It was miserable. I would like to go back there in the heat. Besides, when I went many of the attractions were not yet built. So, for the most part all I recall is that I was forced to decide on chasing pussy to the sugarcane fields of Cuba or staying put in America. You know, maybe if I had made the other choice I too could be teaching at a highbrow American university. I would have settled down and disciplined myself to study diligently and to complete all of my studies toward professorship. Nah, first off I hate reading. Second, I hate discipline. Not a good combo for the scholarly."

Orlando laughed. "The school I am going to go to is called DigiPen. It is the only school in the country for games programmers. Nothing but fat, lonely nerds who love computer games." He stopped talking about school and in the voice of someone who has been terrorized he confessed, "But, Texas, I need to tell you what happened. I wish it was a girlfriend and that I got her pregnant. That would be heavenly compared to what happened. Remember that wacko buddy of mine? The one I call *Cousin It?* The wild man who drinks too much and takes too many drugs? He killed his girlfriend and I drove him there. I didn't know what he was going to do. I never would have taken him. He had promised to buy me a full tank of gas if I gave him a ride and waited for him. He said he just had to give her something and it would only take a few minutes. I waited in the car while he walked inside."

I was stunned and curious. "What the hell?"

"The school is in Washington state and I toured it last summer and decided then and there that I wanted to go there. They have already accepted me. No scholarships, though, so it is going to cost me every nickel that I have saved."

I yelled at Orlando, "Stop bullshiting! Listen kid, I don't care about the damn school right now. Are you being real about this murder? Are you that driver who came to my building? What the hell, are you nuts? Stupid? How can you possibly get involved in a goddamn murder?"

Orlando continued the confession. "I dropped him off at his house and when he got out of the car he spoke very fast and low, telling me that something had gone wrong in her apartment and that he had pushed her a little too hard. That he would keep me out of it but that I would hear about it in the news. Then he walked away. On the drive home I heard a news flash that an apparent murder had taken place. I walked into my room and fell asleep, but woke up pretty fast because I had this dream: a woman, tall, about twenty years old, dark hair, is terrifying me because of what she is doing to a bird. I am on the second floor of a big house that has windows open and no screens. I peek into her room and watch her bashing a pillow against a wall. It is an awful bashing of a pillow. But the noise is louder than a pillow. The noise is reaching underneath the door of the woman's room. I push lightly against the door and the door moves quietly open so that I am witness to the terror of her rage. She is ripping apart a bird as if it were a piece of cotton. I am about to leave and she catches sight of me watching her. Then I woke up with a cold sweat and I knew that I had been screaming. So I jumped out of bed, got dressed, and drove to the police station. *Cousin It* is in custody right now and I am being considered a material witness and a suspect. But they let me go because I came to them and they say that will be in my good graces if they press charges against me. Man, I am so scared."

The only thing I knew to do was to offer the kid some hope. "Orlando. I tell you what. You will get out of this clean. You did right by going to the cops. You could have driven over there a little sooner. But hell kid, you knew nothing about his plans, did you?" Orlando shook his head and held back the tears. "This summer, when we finish this library project, let's go to Disney World. My treat, kid. You deserve it."

"What?"

"Disney World. The Magic Kingdom. My treat, kid."

"Really?"

"Yes. That is if I can ever get you to finish painting. You have got to learn how to talk and paint at the same time."

"I'll work on that." Orlando dipped his brush back into the bucket of paint.

The light on the walls was pouring the color of a future into our eyes and the brightness of hope was mixed into each new brush stroke.

THE BUTTERFLY
GARDEN

The Butterfly Garden

NORA MURPHY
St. Anthony Park

Running down our front steps on her way to basketball practice, Livvy stopped to call out, "Mom, I forgot to tell you. My class is doing community service for the seniors at United Methodist Church. I saw The Porch Man there on Wednesday. At first I didn't recognize him, but I'm sure it's him. He said to say hi."

After Livvy disappeared up Brewster Street, I sat down on our wooden porch swing. It didn't take long to realize that she meant Lars Halvorson. He had given us the swing when he moved out of the old house on Dudley Street. After that, Livvy and I had always called him The Porch Man.

I grew up next door to the Halvorsons up on Dudley. Ingrid Halvorson was like a second mother to me. She fixed me tea in her green porcelain pot; she watched me perform dances on her back porch; she helped me zip my winter jacket trimmed with white fur. Every Christmas she smiled when I showed her the new stuffed animal from my aunt. But once Mrs. Halvorson's disease took root—sculpting her body into a frozen skeleton— she changed from trusted adult into feared ghost.

When the scleroderma advanced and she could no longer sit upright, Lars would carry his wife to the porch swing. The swing filled the afternoons with a slow creak, crying like the crows in the elms. My mother would urge me to go visit Mrs. Halvorson, but the sound of her gasping for breath scared me. I made excuses—like having to take a trip on my bicycle down the hill to return books to the library.

Earlier that morning, Livvy and I walked up to the gardens at Luther Seminary. She wanted to know how to plant a butterfly garden. We studied the one planted there. In the April light, the coneflower, coreopsis, lavender, and butterfly bushes looked more dead than alive. Their faded green shoots stared at the spring sun and dared themselves to grow. I knew Livvy could already see the flowers in full bloom.

As I waited for Livvy to return from basketball, I started correcting a batch of student papers from my honors English class at Central. Between essays, I watched the sun spill across Alden Square. My eyes rested on the white painted gazebo at the eastern end of the little park, which we built with our neighbors when Livvy was a toddler. We drew the plans, obtained the permits, bought the materials, laid the foundation, raised the frame, and set the floor. We stomped the pine slats of the floor in place, varnished the planks, and stomped on them again once they had dried—just to hear our boots thump on the wood.

And we buried a box next to the gazebo. Neighbors filled it with photos, poems, newspaper articles, and assorted scraps of history. Livvy and I contributed a pair of her baby booties—the ones I had knit with little red hearts on them.

When I grew up in St. Anthony Park, I never trusted the love that surrounded me. I still distance myself from family. Yes, I visit my mother every week in the assisted living facility. I still call my brother in Seattle every Christmas. Duty, not choice. I never married and I adopted Livvy from China. Acquaintances no longer ask me where she is from or how she got to St. Paul. But I still ask questions. Where does her optimism come from? Did she bring it with her on her journey across the ocean? Or did she find it through my love?

My parents, both scientists at the university, moved into the house on Dudley with Mother's father after Grandma died. Grandfather Iverson had come from Norway to study at Luther Seminary—with plans to leave on a mission for China. Instead, he married, bought the three-story clapboard house, and never left St. Anthony Park until he died when I was five years old. With Aquavit on his breath, he used to tell me stories about a Norwegian princess. The princess was beautiful, too beautiful. Her father set her on a hill of glass. She had to wait for a prince to climb the fragile slope and rescue her.

My mother had just one older brother. Sig Iverson. He died in World War II. He left behind his stamp collection. Sometimes I'd take it down from the built-in buffet in our living room. My ghost uncle organized his stamps by color—not by country or value. He signed his name in an unruly boy's hand at the bottom of every page.

Grandpa Iverson cried whenever he talked about Uncle Sig. Sometimes he muttered something about the gold star in the front window. I searched for a star but never found one. Years later I learned that families hung a flag with a blue star if they had a son in the service. If the boy died, they replaced the blue star with a gold one.

The windows on Dudley had been graced with four gold stars during World War II. The Robertson twins, my Uncle Sig, and Magnus Halvorson, Lars's older brother. For years, a stone plaque on the library lawn commemorated those who had died. But a few years before I adopted Livvy, the war memorial mysteriously disappeared. No one knew where it had gone. Ghost boys and a ghost stone.

I don't think Livvy knows any ghost stories. She goes to school four blocks from home, plays soccer and basketball at Langford Park, carpools with friends to the Mall of America for movies, and visits the library once a week. Her childhood, full of roaming and exploring, reminds me of my brother Angus.

Angus was best friends with Lars and Ingrid Halvorson's youngest and unexpected son Robby. Robby and Angus spent every free moment together. They played in the Halvorsons' sandbox, gathering up pennies that Mrs. Halvorson hid there. At Halloween they dressed up like twin pirates with matching hooks and eye patches. They played pickup in College Park all summer long—from morning until dinner. As they grew older, they left the park to sneak into the State Fair, bike around Como Lake, and take the bus downtown to trade stamps at the small shop near Rice Park.

Angus had a butterfly collection. Monarchs, red-spotted purples, tiger swallowtails, red admirals, and silver-spotted fritillaries hung in frames on his bedroom wall. Their imprisoned wings had been stopped in mid-flight.

Robby and Angus would walk up to the golf course and lie in wait for butterflies in the tall marshy grasses. They followed them along the abandoned streetcar line out toward the old Gibbs farm. They captured them in the swampy bottoms behind university housing.

At night, Angus used to fill his glass butterfly jar with fireflies—saying, "They are magic fairies dancing just for you." He always let my fairies go, explaining that they had to fly back home. The butterflies weren't so lucky. Angus put them in the glass jar to die. After they suffocated, he pulled them out and mounted them with pins. Sometimes I'd try to watch, but I thought I could hear them crying. I usually turned and ran away.

Angus lives in Seattle now. He's a scientist—like my parents. Maybe we still talk at Christmas every year because there is a part of me that knows that he still holds magic fireflies in his heart. Robby Halvorson lives in Alaska, working as a lawyer. I haven't seen him for years.

I shifted my students' papers on the porch swing. My arm brushed against a jagged bit of wood. I looked down and noticed it was loose. I tugged on the wood and pulled it off. There was a small hole with a piece of paper tucked inside it. I unfolded the paper and discovered a poem written in blue ink.

Your eyes are as bright
As the moon on the lake.
Your lips are as red as

The sugar maple in fall.
Promise me that you'll
Wait for me, my dear.
My own sweet moon maple,
For I'm forever yours.

The Halvorsons wrote each other love poems? Robby's parents? Those frail, feared ghosts?

Before school the following Wednesday I put the Halvorsons' poem into a manila envelope and scratched out a short note on the back:

Dear Mr. Halvorson,

I found this in the old porch swing this weekend. My daughter Livvy will return it to you at the senior lunch today. I hope you enjoy reading it again.

Faith Saunders
667 Brewster Street

P.S. Will Robby be at the Murray reunion this year?

"Livvy," I scolded, "don't you dare forget this package. You're doing double community service today. Mr. Halvorson will want what's in here."

It was difficult to concentrate in the classroom that day. I wished I could see the smile on Mr. Halvorson's face when he read the old poem. I wanted to watch him transform into Ingrid Halvorson's lover. Livvy had basketball practice after school, so I had to wait until dinner to ask about her delivery.

"Well, he gave me a funny look when he opened it. I mean, he was polite," explained Livvy, "but when he looked at it he just crinkled up his face— almost like he was gonna cry. Then he handed it back and said good-bye."

"He gave it back? Where is it now?"

"In my backpack."

"Go get it. Please."

When Livvy returned with the envelope, I pulled out the old poem and stared at the handwriting.

Neither of the Halvorsons had written it.

Of course Mr. Halvorson didn't write it—he has always made a point of writing in black ink, like his father, whose fountain pen he had inherited. The poem was written in blue ink. The words leaned to the left and the s's fell slightly below the line. Mrs. Halvorson's script leaned to the right and she wrote like she spoke—when she still could—chipper and on the up-and-up, not below the lines.

I prefer stories to facts. When I was twelve, my father told me, "Faith, if you're smart, you will stop reading all those novels and dedicate yourself to finding answers—not more questions. Begin, for example, with the laws of thermodynamics."

He continued, "Energy cannot be destroyed, my dear. It can only be transformed." Then he gestured from the clouds to the dew on the grass. "You may thank me one day, Faith."

I had never believed my father until a week after the recent poem fiasco. I'm not sure "grateful" is the word I'd use to describe what happened. Livvy and I sat down for dinner. She had her backpack with her.

"Mom, one of the old ladies at the church today said she knew you. I can't remember her name, but she said she worked up at the university with Grandma."

"What's her name?"

"I don't know. Mr. Halvorson came up and they started talking before I could ask."

"The Porch Man returneth?"

"Yeah, and then he gave me this. He said it's for you."

Livvy dug out a small box wrapped in white tissue paper. She set it on the kitchen table. There was a note taped on top of the box, written in Mr. Halvorson's familiar black fountain pen.

Dear Faith,

I've been meaning to return this to you for some time and apologize for the delay. The last time Robby was in town he told me that this belonged to your brother Angus. I hope you enjoy this memento of your childhood.

It's been a pleasure getting to know your daughter at the Wednesday luncheons. She reminds me of you—a helpful and kind child, but perhaps a bit less dreamy. I hope you are well. Please send my regards to your mother.

Sincerely,

Lars Halvorson
1825 Carter

I set the letter down and ripped off the tissue paper. Inside the box, my hands hit something hard and square. Smooth on one side, like glass, and rough on the other—wood. Keeping my eyes half-closed, I pulled out Mr. Halvorson's gift. It was one of my brother's prize butterfly frames.

A regal orange-black monarch spread its wings in perfect symmetry in the center. At the upper left a smaller tiger swallowtail sat with its antennae pointed up, almost touching the glass surface. In the lower right the eyes of a red admiral shined in the reflection of the kitchen light.

I wish I hadn't been able to recognize it. This particular frame was the centerpiece of the collection Angus had submitted for the tenth-grade butterfly competition in Mr. Ridder's science class. If I turned the frame over I knew I would see his name burned into the wood with my father's old

wood drill. *Angus Saunders, 1967*. I fingered the grooves as I tried to answer
Livvy's questions.

"Why did Mr. Halvorson give this to you?"

"They . . . they are your Uncle Angus's butterflies."

"Really? Can I have them?"

Though I wanted to say no, I handed the framed trio over to Livvy.

All spring and into the summer, Livvy and I continued to work on the garden
in Alden Square. We dug the earth, turning it up into the warming air. We
planted seeds and starter plants. The neighbors waved to us on their way to
work as we hauled our watering cans across the street to the garden. Evening
inspections brought out curious toddlers, students, and seniors who shared
their opinions with us—which plants would flower first, what kind of fertilizer
was best, whether the butterflies would eat their tomato crops on their way to
our new garden. But everyone shared one common dream—we all hoped
that the butterflies would arrive by the Fourth of July. Livvy knew they would.

St. Anthony Park knows how to celebrate the Fourth. At the heart of
our celebration is a parade followed by an evening supper. The parade
starts at the seminary lawns, works its way up the hill past the shops, and
down the steep incline elbowing by United Methodist Church and into
Langford Park. It involves the entire neighborhood—half of us watching
and the other half marching. Volunteers push senior citizens in wheel-
chairs. Grown men ride lawn mowers. Younger men carry lawn chairs.
Political dignitaries march alongside neighborhood fixtures like the
butcher from Sir Speedy Market. Children on bikes—hundreds of children and grandchildren who get toted back to the old neighborhood for
the day—make up the rear of the parade. Afterwards, children play games
while the adults set up for the chicken dinner and prep the stage for
speeches and live music.

On the day of the Fourth, Livvy and I nestled onto our blanket on the park lawn for another St. Anthony Park tradition—listening to the winning sixth-grade essay, "Being an American." This year Livvy's friend Pakoua had won. She leaned into me and whispered, "I told you she'd win the contest, didn't I? Even you wouldn't have put a single red mark on her essay."

After the speeches, Livvy and I headed for opposite sides of the chicken stand. She joined Pakoua in line for dinner and I joined faithful Mrs. Boler—head chef for more than twenty years now. I scooped coleslaw onto paper plates, smiling at everyone. The bluegrass band started and I tapped my big metal spoon in time to the music. Livvy and her friends stood across the park in a big huddle, forming a mirror image of a group of boys on the other side of a cottonwood. As I turned my attention back to the coleslaw, a latecomer approached the stand.

"Good evening, Faith."

"Mr. Halvorson," I managed. "It's great to . . . to . . . I'm sorry."

"No, I apologize. I shouldn't have held on to your brother's prize for so long. Robby's not coming back to Minnesota was a poor excuse on my part."

"Not at all," I replied.

"How's your mother?"

"Not great, to be honest. Cancer's back. Spread. She doesn't have long. She will probably go quickly—like my father did."

"I'm sorry."

I struggled to say something else.

"Faith, I have another memento for you. Could I bring it by your house tomorrow morning?"

"Of course. Come and see our new garden in Alden Square. Livvy and I are usually out watering by about 8:30."

It was hot the next day. Neither Livvy nor I minded the feel of the cool water spilling over the edges of our watering cans, trickling down our legs and over our flip-flops. When Lars arrived, we were just finishing up. He had a brown paper grocery bag from Sir Speedy Market with him. He stooped with fatigue, as if the contents of the bag were heavy.

I invited him over to the house for a cup of coffee. He waited on the front porch. From the kitchen I could hear the swing creak. When I returned to the front porch the swing was empty except for the brown bag. He was halfway out the front door.

"Faith, I want you to have what's in the bag. Please keep it for me, for our families."

"Certainly, Mr. Halvorson. Won't you stay for that cup of coffee?"

He had already made his way down the front steps and onto the street—his gait faster and posture straighter than when he had arrived. I waved and turned to open the bag.

I pulled out a piece of rugged, black-speckled rock—heavy considering its size, about four by six inches. I turned the rock over and read two names engraved in gold lettering. Magnus Halvorson. Sig Iverson.

I realized that the granite was from the missing war memorial that used to stand on the library lawn. What took me longer to figure out was why Mr. Halvorson had given me the rock.

Then it hit me.

All at once I saw my Uncle Sig's signature in his old stamp collection. It was in the same handwriting as the poem. I had finally found the poet.

My Uncle Sig had written the love poem to Ingrid Halvorson. He had given it to her before he left for the war. It said, "Promise me that you'll wait." She did not. She married Lars Halvorson, yet she kept Sig's poem hidden in the porch swing. Mr. Halvorson couldn't bear holding on to this cold stone.

"Mom! Come here! Mom!"

"What, Livvy?"

"The frame—the butterflies. They're gone."

I walked into Livvy's bedroom and asked, "What are you talking about?"

I picked up Angus's frame. The glass wasn't broken, but the butterflies no longer lay on the black canvas. Had the Norwegian prince finally come to rescue the butterflies from their glass prison?

Livvy and I heard laughter outside. We walked back to the front porch. Children were playing in Livvy's garden. I opened the screen door and watched them running through the flowers. The children were chasing three butterflies.

ELEVEN WAYS
TO LIVE IN THE CITY

Eleven Ways to Live in the City

JOANNA RAWSON
Merriam Park

I.

Rollin was just off the late shift, headed home down the alley on foot. When he reached the backyard of the Autumn Manor Apartment House he looked up and saw his own kitchen light on. That's strange, he thought, I *never* leave that light on. He climbed the stairs and knocked lightly, not wanting to startle whoever was in there. A woman with her hair up in blue rollers answered. Rollin explained that he lived there, that in fact he had lived there for some twenty years, so she let him in. A teenage boy with admirable piercings was thumbing through Rollin's record albums, mostly vintage jazz session stuff. "Dude, no Moby?" "Sorry, my friend," Rollin said, then asked his hostess if she might like to offer him a beer. The three of them sat down together on the couch. Rollin's cat curled at their feet. By the time the sun came up, they'd all gotten acquainted and, after finding little in common, confessed their most guilty secrets to one another in the wee hours. No one's revelations struck any of them as demonic or surprising. Their camaraderie felt immensely right, then Rollin got up to make eggs and coffee. When it started to rain he lent the pair his umbrella, trusting in its return.

2.

An hour before the wedding, two cars crashed at the intersection of Ashland and Griggs. The Integra lodged sideways around a tree trunk and the Yugo was sent flying onto the Hacketts' lawn. Mr. H., not three feet from ground zero, stripped off his tux jacket and squatted down to assess the damage. "Lordy, there's a baby in there!" he said. Mr. H. reached in and unfastened the little human from its five-point security seat. The youngster, a girl, appeared to be unscathed and flashed the wedding party a toothless grin. The ambulance arrived soon after and idled amidst the shattered glass and gawkers. "Sure is a shame the driver of this Integra won't make it," the EMT said before racing off with his cargo, "but basically you couldn't ask for a more judicious outcome under the circumstances." Who could argue? Not the minister, who wed the young couple as scheduled while the bride's mother cradled the foundling in her arms and cooed. St. Paul's finest were still conducting an inch-by-inch search of the scene when the cake was served, but they never did locate a driver for the Yugo. The tow truck came and hauled it from the azalea bed. The authorities cleared out. The newly-weds drove off, waving, with a trail of tin cans tied to the bumper. To Mr. H. it seemed as if the Lordy had come through again. He and Mrs. H. tucked their new daughter into bed that night in the room of the old, married daughter who was now lost to them. In the morning he found a road map of Oahu in the shrubbery. The next spring, at bloom time, he found a size seven beige pump and a rearview mirror. Those were the only clues.

3.

Velma went off her meds a week ago and woke up the following morning with a start. She felt fresh as a daisy. "Time to make that quilt!" She had been born in a cave overlooking the Mississippi, with a barrier set up to keep the pigs at bay and no plumbing, just a crapper in the corner. That was eighty-odd years in the past, down in Swede's Hollow, and Velma had been collecting fabric ever since. Lately, her basement was full of cloth from bygone days: kitchen curtains, the kids' prom dresses, coverlets, her once highly regarded afro slacks. She'd meant to turn them all into something unified long ago. Velma got cracking at dawn. She set up the old

Singer on the porch, spun the bobbin, adjusted the tension, and embarked. Days went by. She ate next to nothing, mostly sardines and cider. It didn't occur to her to sleep. She was possessed of an industrious and daunting spirit. I stopped by unannounced earlier today and found Velma wide awake, somewhere in the folds of a quilt that easily could have covered the roof. She was going strong. Her fingers were on fire. When I offered her some relief from the trusty vials in my bag, she graciously refused by quoting scripture. It was then I noticed the aural glow emanating from her person, not unlike the light illuminating certain figures by Rembrandt.

4.

Last Tuesday I stopped off at the Crescenterra Towers on my way home from bowling, which I prefer to do in the afternoons, solo. I greeted Hortense, the receptionist, with my usual salute and took a seat in the community room by the window. St. Mark's Parish stood across the street, a lonely ode to fine masonry. It is here that Nelson and I while away the dead time before twilight. He shuffled over and recounted his two-year tour of duty in Nam, as he is wont to do each week. On this particular day the perfume of lilacs in high bloom purpled the air as he ticked down the geopolitical surveillance skills he had acquired in the jungle. Later, I've been told, he proved to be quite an asset in the security field: sleuthing corporate graft, tracking errant wives, etc., until his time-delayed ticker went berserk. They wheeled him over to the towers and ensconced him on the twenty-third floor, with a parakeet. We talk on Tuesdays. I tell Nelson that I am a certified psychiatrist. This is a lie, though I feel justified in repeating it each time we meet, as I believe it helps him to trust me. He sits still mostly, with just his mouth going, while the world moves from right to left as if he were reading it on a page. We have yet to agree on the exact language in which it is written.

5.

My husband kept going to jail for bad checks and drinking. During these disappearing acts I had four kids. You might ask how. He'd get out, I'd get knocked up, he'd go back in. It's that simple—a natural order of things. Why'd he keep going in? I have three theories: 1. He liked it in there. 2. He liked doing what he did to get in there too much to stop. 3. He was trying to get away from me and his growing brood. In the years since he was murdered, I've ruled out the first two mainly because, for one, my husband would constantly get disfigured in the slammer (being such a little runt with a big mouth and the sort of presence that inspires bullying), and who would like that? And, on the second count, because he suffered such remorseful guilt about his crimes as only a former altarboy can (this put the preemptive crimp on the fun in his sprees). So it must have been the latter—me and the kids. You will not find other animals in the kingdom behaving as he did against his own. He was not redeemed during his detentions; no, I believe he was made worse by them. Why, our last child looks exactly like Dick Nixon.

6.

I am Rigby the Boxer, a champion, twice-belted, master of the TKO and subliminal domination, hailing from the Bahamas, now of Frogtown, St. Paul, a triumphant specimen, of ironlike torso and rippled about the pecs with disciplined musculature, maker of lesser men into tomato cans and beggars and pulp, immune to mercy on the ropes, a southpaw, a sought-after sparrer, certified for the public match, featherweight, fleet of footwork and a fright, purply enrobed, deluxely sponsored, laced up, slicked down, a phoenix of the fight, debatably mortal, divine against all ill, I, Rigby, about to embark on a vow of speechlessness, who have studied the motions of the non-talker and found in them inspiration beyond the once beautiful, now merely brutal machinations of the ring, do hereby declare my pending utterly mute state to have now commenced. Farewell, eloquence. Hello, silence, the sweetest science of all.

7.

My friend Angela phoned and asked did I want to go spy on her boyfriend—
see if he was fooling around on her. It was an evening with little else to do,
so why not. We parked two blocks away, by the Lulu Food Mart & Deli, and
snuck up under his window, but there was nothing doing inside, just him
on the bed reading comic books. When we got back to the car I sat on the
front bumper. It was a '55 Chevy, light blue. Angela turned on the motor
and reached over to open my door, but I guess she put her foot on the gas
instead of the brake. I slipped off but my sweater hooked on and I got
dragged. She was screaming and I was screaming but the car didn't stop. We
were on a hill, it was paved over and also had oil and gravel. Pretty much all
my skin ripped off. The priest gave me last rites in the hospital six times. A
year later, Angela asked me to be in her wedding. She was getting married
to that same high-school sweetheart, the non-cheater. The dress she picked
for her bridal party was a halter style—no sleeves, lots of cleavage, high
thigh slit, same powder blue as the car—so all my scarring showed. In the
photographs, the grafts look like boiled ham. Angela calls my skin the reason he proposed. In her Christmas card every year she still thanks me.

8.

Some nights I come to in the zinnia patch. Others, in the corner phone
booth by the Grandview Theater, in mid-dial to the emergency room. My
name is Irv and I am a sleepwalker. I have been to meetings for help and gotten none. My condition has evolved into an eschatological riddle after these
fifty-three years of nocturnal suffering. I fall asleep easily enough. I make it
through midnight undisturbed. It is the wee hours at the end of night that
trouble the soul and make the body rise. A witness (my ex-wife) studied the
stirrings and could not penetrate their system of trance and tic. Even after
clinical observation, the cause of my doings remains a mystery. I have gone
naked in winter to the neighbors' house, and knocked. I have driven cars,

once to a tent revival by the river, most recently to a long-term corporate file storage warehouse on Clark Street. Asleep, in motion, I am a force unburdened by desires or will. I must be reckoned with. This predicament must end before someone is hurt or worse. I wake up making noises that aren't mine and know not where I am, or what.

9.

Frank started drinking at noon while his wife Gertrude was still at church. She came home from Good Shepherd Lutheran to get the pot roast ready for visitors and scolded him for being sloshed. "You're a damn mess," she told him, and he agreed. "Now get down to the cellar and bring me a jar of that aspic I canned. Helen and the others are on their way over." His wooden leg made a noise going down that brought Clydesdales to mind. Gertrude busied herself. By sunset he still hadn't come up. She'd fed the company. She'd washed the roaster. She'd hung the wash out back. What in the world? she thought when it was time for bed and Frank still hadn't emerged. Yes, he'd gotten his suspenders tangled in the rafters, but that was mid-after-noon and he'd managed to boing free. And yes, he'd later been involved in the late sixties back issues of *National Geographic* over by the defunct incinera-tor. But it was midnight and still no Frank. Gertrude slept straight through the night for the first time in years, dreaming about seagulls.

10.

Granny died last year and left me these directions for washing clothes. 1. Build fire in backyard to heet kittle of rain water. 2. Set tubs so smoke won't blow in eyes if wind is pert. 3. Shave one hole cake of lie soap in bilin water. 4. Sort things, make 3 piles—1 white, 1 cullard, 1 work britches and rags. 5. Stir flour in cold water to smooth, then thin down with bilin water. 6. Rub dirty spots on board, scrub hard, then bile. Rub cullard, don't bile, just rench in starch. 7. Take white things out of kittle with broomstick handle, then rench, blew, and starch. 8. Spread tea towels on grass. 9. Hang old rags on fence. 10. Pore rench water in flour bed. 11. Scrub porch with hit soapy water. 12. Turn tubs upside down. 13. Go put on clean dress, smooth hair with side combs, brew cup of tea, set and rest and count your blessins. That's it, Granny's secret method. I hung this up above my automatic washer and I read it when things look bleak.

II.

For kicks my next-door neighbor likes to cruise around town dressed as a cop. He trolls down Snelling Avenue, he snakes up Marshall. He surveys the fairgrounds in summer, he investigates the Winter Carnival downtown. He drives this black Crown Vic he bought off the auction block and has since sweetened up with decorative chrome plating, large antennae, a radar on the dash, supplemental red lights, a PA system, and so on. Sometimes late at night I see him out in the yard, pretending to arrest trees. He'll pat one down as if he's been trained in procedures. He'll slap a fake ticket on the oak. Once he cuffed a larch. After that brutal incident, I asked him, "Hey, what's the idea with this get-up?" "The law," he replied, "is nine-tenths of every-thing." I offered him a julep and he accepted, saying he wasn't due at the sta-tion house for another hour. "But really," I pressed, "you're not a cop. You'll never be a cop. Why torture yourself with this charade?" He thought about that as if he'd thought about it before, then said, "We're in more danger than ever. Strange little monks in deceptive orange robes and Reeboks lurk at the bus stop. Kids on prom night with their pierced nipples stick their tattoed heads out the sunroofs of limos. Female synchronized swimmers pirouette in the rooftop pools of tittie bars. On my beat I have seen it all. I offer myself as an agent against evil. It is for the good of the free world that I persist."

FROM ONE WINDOW

From One Window

JULIA KLATT SINGER
Highland Park

My mother said, "Eleanor. That's a beautiful name. That's my daughter's name. She was lovely, but she had a bit of a temper when she wasn't the center of attention. You know the type."

I tried not to cry. I tried not to breathe. The scream sat in my throat until I could force it back down. I didn't picture it ending up in my stomach, where it could be digested. More likely it would end up in my liver or kidney, someplace where it could turn to stone. Even though the nurse warned me that my mother might not remember who I was, I never really believed her. I'm her only daughter, her oldest child. She has known me my entire life.

"And it is so nice of you to call on me. Can I get you some tea?" She sat in her pale yellow chintz chair that seemed to hold the morning sun. It was the last real piece of furniture in the living room. She was dressed in hose and a navy button-down dress. She looked confident. Capable. I accepted the tea.

Following her into the kitchen, I noticed that the movers had already been there. The dining room was empty, except for three boxes: one with my brother's name, Isaac, on it, and two with mine—big firm letters, the kind a first grader makes while the teacher looks over her shoulder—ELEANOR. The kitchen table was gone, as were the chairs. The teakettle was still on the stove top and I could see two cups in the drainer. Those would move with her.

"I'm having a little work done on the place. So some nice young men came and cleaned the rooms for me. Sweet of them, isn't it?"

"You're moving, aren't you?" I wanted to say "Mother" but couldn't form the word.

"Only for a little while. I just thought I'd make it easier on the painters. They like to paint in peace. Artists always need their space." She raised her eyebrows and smiled. "So I'm going on vacation. I hope to visit my mother and my sister. They've been gone a while now and I really must catch up with them. I think they're at our summer place, in the south of France. The tea will only take a minute." She picked up the kettle from the back burner, then set it down again.

She stood then, facing the window that overlooks Summit Avenue. All my life I remember her standing there just like that; gazing, waiting, lost in thought. Two women in their fifties, a little younger than me I suppose, walked by with such purpose, as if walking were the only important thing in their lives. I filled the kettle with water and turned on the stove. There was a box of Lipton in the cupboard. I wished I had remembered to bring her some good English tea.

My keys were wrapped around my index finger, lying in the palm of my hand. I couldn't put them down. It used to drive her crazy, the way I held on to them. "Always looks like you're about to run for the door," she'd complain. She doesn't notice them anymore. Only when I'm at home do I let go of them, hanging them on the hook near the phone. My husband thinks I'm a little obsessed about losing things.

The key ring is small and gold, just a little larger than my thumb. It fits neatly on my finger, almost like a regular ring. I have four keys on it. My house key, my mother's house key, the key to my car, and a small brass key that I no longer remember what it's for, but can't bring myself to discard. Maybe because it's a key that looks and feels exactly like a key should. Mother's key will stay on the ring too, even after she's moved.

I wandered back to the living room and sat down on the folding chair near the card table in the center of the room. The estate sale people had used it while selling off the household things that neither Isaac nor I could deal with. I could hear my mother humming, waiting for the kettle to whistle. She was still standing, staring out the kitchen window. Empty, the living room felt bigger. I wondered if that is how Mother feels, inside her head, now that the memories are lost, the past a jumble of words, names, objects unattached to anything, anyone. I pictured kites with broken strings, balloons floating free, getting smaller and smaller with each blink of an eye. A whole life's worth of memories and knowledge, definitions and sums drifting off.

She brought the tea to the living room on a tray and set it carefully on the cardboard table. I opened the box of good Belgium chocolates that I had brought for her.

"You remembered! You remembered how much I love chocolate!" She clapped her hands together like a child.

"Try one. They're delicious." I handed her the box.

"Heavenly. Don't tell Mother. She'd never approve of chocolate so close to dinner." Her hands looked exactly as I remember them. The veins prominent and strong, her fingers long and sure.

I promised not to tell.

"And I have something for you," she said.

I wondered who I was to her, and what it might be that she had for me.

"Another treat. Since we're misbehaving." She headed to the dining room. I heard the doors to the built-in hutch creak open, then click closed. She entered the room carrying a jug. It looked like it weighed half as much as she did.

"You must try this. Just a sip. It's the best there is. My family has been in the wine making business for years. My sisters and I picked the grapes from the time we could walk."

She set the jug down on the table, headed to the kitchen, and returned with two juice glasses and a small pitcher of water. The jug was made of brown pottery with a small handle at the neck and an aged cork. I had heard the story of wine making in France a thousand times, but I had never seen this jug before.

Popping the cork off, she poured an inch into each of the glasses.

"We'll need to water it a bit. It's nearly as old as I am. Been around since Prohibition," she said with a wink. "Please, have a drink." She lifted her glass and closed her eyes, brought the glass to her nose and sniffed. I saw in her the young woman she once was, the practiced line of a hostess, the easy smile. She'd told me once, long ago, about how her father sold bootleg for a time. I had stumbled across a photograph from the early twenties. She was four or five, sitting next to her mother on a horse-drawn wagon. Her younger sister, Louisa, just a baby then, was perched on Grandmother Pachett's knee. Grandmother Pachett wore a long skirt and fitted jacket. The reins lay loose in her hands. On the back it read, "Return run from Osceola, Wisc." She told me about how there were jugs of bootleg under the bench seat, under her mother's skirt. No officer of the law would make a woman lift her skirt, not in those days, anyway, she had said.

"After you. I have two kids and a husband who'll be home and wanting dinner soon," I told her.

"Ah—I'd never let that stop me from having a little fun." She poured a splash of water into the wine and sipped it. It was dark red, like blood, even with the water in it. Smacking her lips she said, "Better than I remember it! Just like being with a man."

I took the two boxes home, wondering what Mother had set aside for me. Inside one was her tin of loose buttons. As a girl I had loved playing with the buttons. There were buttons from Papa's work shirts, white with four holes, buttons from jackets, dresses, and shirts that she had snipped off after the garment no longer fit or was beyond wear. I loved the black velvet-covered buttons from Mother's fancy dress, and the wooden toggles that I remembered stuffing through the holes of my first school jacket.

There were small yellow, pale blue, and pink buttons from baby clothes long ago turned into rags.

Under the button tin was her silverware. Simple, with a fleur-de-lis at the end. It was the silverware we used on Sundays and holidays. Under the silver, wrapped in a sampler stitched with her girlhood name, Sophia Maria Pachett, was her cookbook. Handwritten recipes for elderberry wine, quiche, and quick apple pies—pies I remember taking all day to make and just a few minutes to devour.

The second box held the wooden stool she had kept in the pantry, along with the brown jug of wine. I set up my tripod and snapped three photos of myself and the jug. I knew that my long, too-thin body and my rash of flaming red hair contrasted well with the plain brown jug. And I wondered if perhaps I'd have been happier if I had been shorter, plumper, less noticeable, more like the jug.

My skin is too thin. Redheads have skin like the belly of a fish. Clear, nearly transparent. Skin that never seems to cover what's happening inside. When I'm angry or hurt, I feel like a clock—its works exposed—ticking out of control.

Isaac has Mother's skin. Almost olive, they both tan easily, even in the winter sun. It's from living so close to the border of Italy as little girl, Mother always said. But they are decidedly French. They wear their skin like clothing, as only the French can. Whatever is going on in their heads or hearts has to be expressed in words, gestures. Their skin reveals nothing, only reflects the light, the mood of the setting they're in.

Later that day, I went to pick up the photos. They weren't ready, so I waited on a bench, across the street from the Walgreens that used to be a Bridgeman's Ice Cream. I kissed Leo Hartmen on the cheek one Saturday night in 1959 after having a strawberry malt where the deodorants, toothpaste, and dental floss are now sold. And before that it was a little restaurant my mother used to go to, The Squeeze Inn. Five tables and a counter, it was famous for its roast beef sandwich with horseradish, and its steamy windows. She and her mom and pop and two sisters went there every Friday night. Grandpop was a salesman and even during the Depression he thought it looked good to keep spending. People didn't trust a salesman who never spent a dime himself. Mother used to flirt with the single men who ate at the counter. The place was so tight, she said, they were practically sitting at her table anyway.

I'd have rather kissed Leo Hartmen there.

My daughter Audrey was across the street in one of those new trendy shops, buying new things that look like old things. I told her she could have my martini shaker, I didn't have much use for it, but she was pretty sure I'd want to keep it. Maybe she was right. Maybe a good stiff martini was what I needed. Mother had just moved into the new place—if you could call it "in."

"What are the pictures of?" Audrey asked when they were finally ready. We'd been waiting an extra fifteen minutes in Walgreens, looking through the Hallmark cards. Audrey likes to read them. She's told me that the secret to a good marriage is communication and that she sends her husband a card every week. They've been married three months now. She met him in a Starbucks. There are worse places, I guess. Like Walgreens. The men at the photo counter are just younger versions of the old men checking their pulse and picking up prescriptions at the pharmacy in the back of the store. I stuffed the pictures in the center compartment of my purse with my wallet and said, "Your grandmother's world."

"Jesus Mom, what did you take pictures of, bedpans and mothballs?"

I've always marveled at my daughter's quick, direct tongue. Since she could talk, she's always said whatever comes into her head. I changed the subject. "How's Ted?"

"He wants to be called Theo now. Thinks it sounds more accomplished. His mother still calls him Teddy. In public. Can you believe it?"

I could, but I didn't say so.

"He's thinking about writing a book. About coffee."

"Really? Sounds like a hot topic."

"It wouldn't be about coffee, but about how coffee is there whenever life is happening. Coffee like air. Or water. Those things we take for granted. You know, I'm the inspiration for the book—after coffee, that is. He said if it hadn't been for coffee, Starbucks coffee, we wouldn't have ever met. He's thinking of contacting Starbucks about the book idea. They may want to publish it."

The taste of the dry smoky wine Mother and I had drunk yesterday returned to my mouth. For a fleeting moment, I considered offering Audrey a drink. But I could already hear her response. Somewhere in there would be a question about who has lost their mind, me or my mother.

The photos turned out better than I had expected. I had used my automatic camera. It was in my purse and it wasn't until after drinking some of the wine that the idea had come to me. I was afraid to leave mother's house without a first batch. Four or five of them were good enough to enlarge. It was a place to start.

Isaac found the new place for mother. It was large and sunny, a corner unit with four rooms and high ceilings. It was nothing like her house on Summit, which had more rooms than you could count, grand built-ins, and windows like picture frames. But it was nice. Her kitchen table, bed, nightstand, and dresser made the move, as did her stereo and yellow chair. Her favorite books were on a new bookshelf and Isaac had to repeatedly explain the microwave to her.

It hadn't gone well. She called me the first night in a panic because she couldn't find her bathroom. I told her to walk from room to room, calmly, that she would find it. She'd spotted a toilet hours ago, she hissed into the phone, but it wasn't *her* bathroom. I hung up and called the nurse hotline that worked with her building. They said it was normal. That sometimes it takes a little while to adjust. Along with the forgetting there'd be anger. There'd be a mess or two to clean up.

She had always been happy on Summit. Yes, there was the time last summer when she forgot to turn the burner off after heating water for tea, and then set the newspaper down on it, but I canceled the paper and she hadn't done anything like that since. But Isaac was having trouble sleeping. He kept picturing Mother lying in a heap at the bottom of some stairway in that rambling house. There were thirteen, he said. Thirteen possible staircases she could fall down. And four bathtubs she could drown in. And now that she was forgetting things, he pictured robbers walking through an open front door at midnight, and Mother in her robe offering them a drink. He'd driven by the house a few times at four A.M. just to make sure it looked fine. So I agreed. It was time for Mother to move.

Of course she was angry. She's losing her mind, and now everything that she knew well had either been sold, taken from her, or rearranged to fit a smaller, more convenient life. She had lived in the house on Summit since 1946. More than half of her life. I was four, and she was pregnant when they moved in. That baby sister died, two days old, as did the next one. All the neighbors had left casseroles, salads, and cakes. When Isaac was born in 1948, they left knitted booties and blankets, boxes of chocolates for her, and cigars for Daddy. She had one or two miscarriages after Isaac was born. Each left a sadness in her eyes, took an inch from her stature. Each one kept Daddy at the office a little later. When he died nearly a decade ago, it didn't surprise me that his heart was the first thing to go.

Through fifty years of marriage, countless dinner parties and open houses, the house was her stage. Each room was carefully decorated to set the proper tone. Mother knew what colors and fabrics to combine to create mood, drama, a sense of comfort and importance.

I put the pictures in simple frames, 12" x 18", and oriented them east to west. There was Summit Avenue—midmorning, the apple tree in bloom to the east of the house, a view of the elm and the sidewalk, a glimpse of the Victorian house to the west I'll always call the Vanderlong's, a picture of the lilacs blooming, the porch chair and rail out back, the green shady back-yard, the carriage house, the vegetable garden with its rows of lettuce and peas. Each was taken from a window of her house. Each is a view she's seen thousands of times before. Isn't that what life is? A thousand views from one window, the glass panes worn from rain, the sills dusty, the paint cracking and peeling, revealing color from long before?

Mother and Isaac came into the living room as I was hanging the third picture. My back was turned to them. I pounded in the nail, a sound much like Mother's footsteps as she enters a room. It was quiet when I tapped the final tap. I turned. I saw her standing and gazing at the picture of Summit Avenue, a car rolling by, the houses across the street. Early spring, it is loaded with color, loaded with promise. She stood, back straight, chin up, arms hanging limply at her sides. Her face was soft, without expression. Isaac looked stunned. Neither I, nor he, nor Mother moved.

"Mrs. Richardson was just telling me the other day that her oldest girl, Mary Kate, is going to have a baby. You remember Mary Kate."

"Yes, Mother. I do remember Mary Kate. What do you remember about her?"

"She always had skinned knees and needed a Band-Aid. And now she's going to have a baby. Isn't that exciting!"

It was, I replied.

"I do hope she has a girl. There's nothing in the world quite like a daughter. Oh, darling, I've forgotten your name, but can I get you some tea? This nice gentleman here was fixing the stove. It shouldn't take him much longer, he keeps insisting it's quite simple to use. Frankly, I think there's a piece or two missing—either in that little stove, or . . ." She smiled at Isaac. "A good cup of tea is the perfect test."

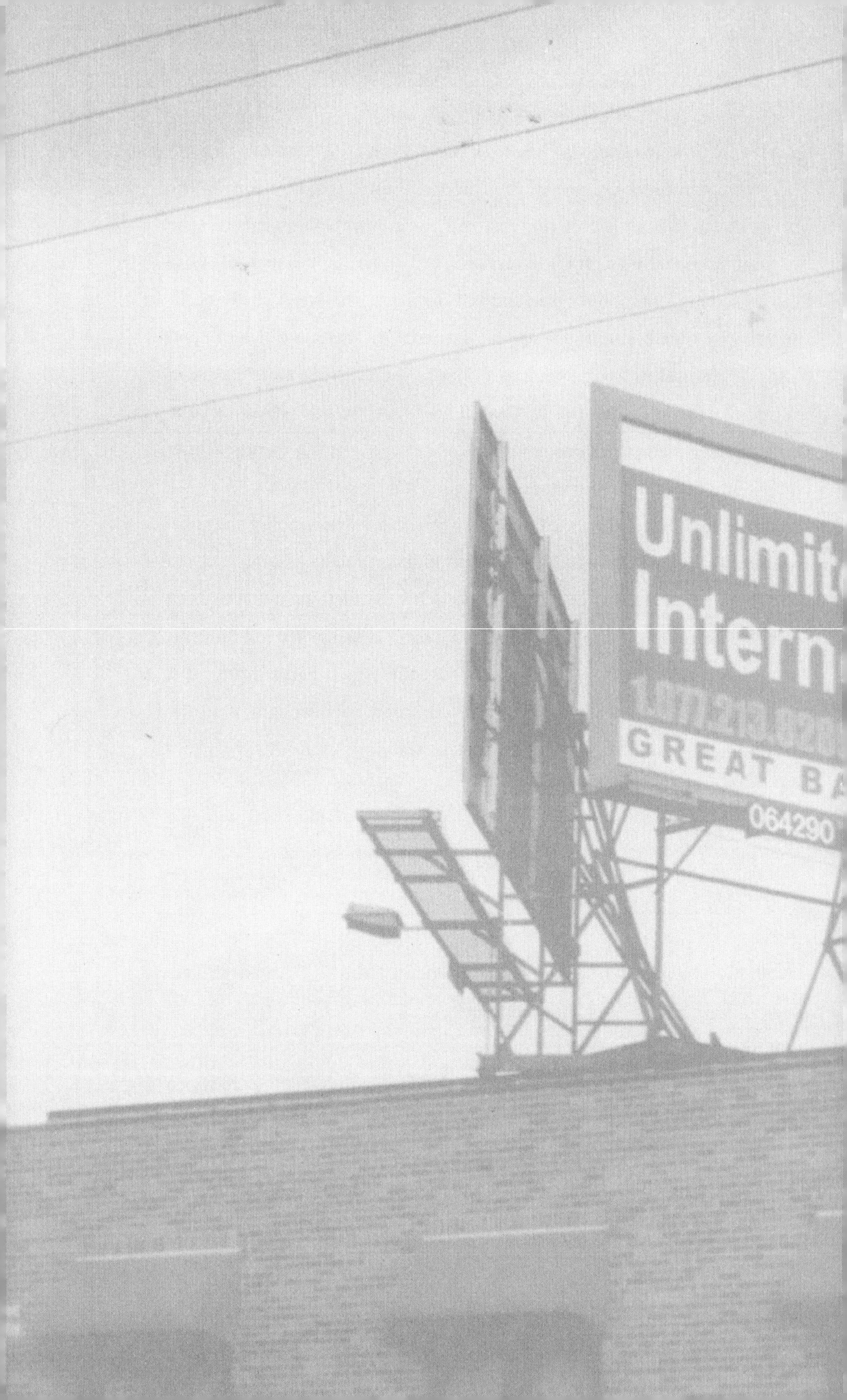
Unlimit
Intern
GREAT BA
064290

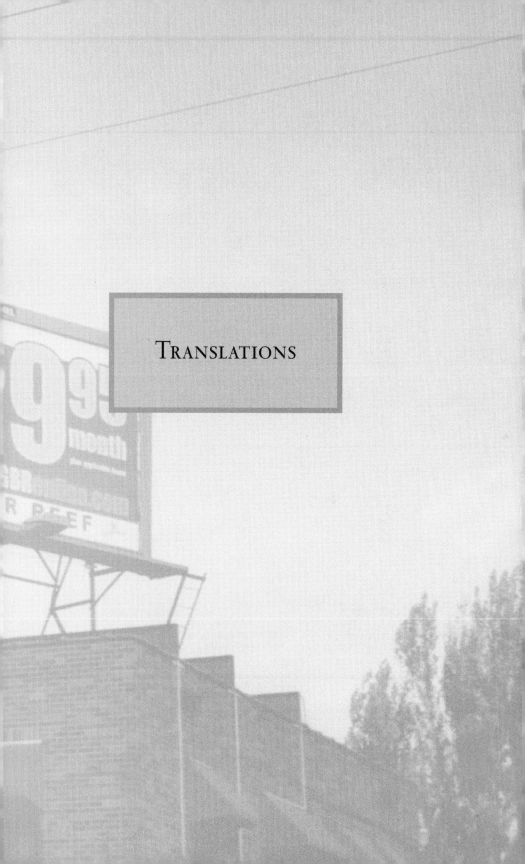

TRANSLATIONS

Translations

JULIA KLATT SINGER

Hamline Midway

My father says the difference between Cambodia and America is like the difference between the ground and the sky. He knew the ground in Cambodia. Farming rice, he was as much a part of the ground as were the rice paddies he worked. Sometimes I dream about Cambodia: dreams dense like the jungle, green and fragrant, filled with the smell of heat, flowers, fire, and blood. Sometimes I dream I am a boy again, and I'm watching my father walk the ox, harvesting the rice. I wake up tired after those dreams, as if I was the one swinging the scythe, planting and harvesting the rice, trying to keep my family alive.

America is like the sky. So big and so visible. It's there in front of us, but impossible to get our hands on. We all reach for things. My father struggles to learn the English words that would make his life easier. My wife Saqui is studying, once again, to be a nurse. She was one of the best in Phnom Penh, and now, at forty-five, she must compete with the young nursing students, she who nursed injuries that these young men and women could never fathom. My son Kor, now eighteen, just wants to be accepted, to blend in, to be American. His friends all call him Kory. Sokka at sixteen wants to stand out, and her twin brother Hauly reminds me the most of myself, wanting to set his own course, to make his own way.

We live in the Bluebird Apartments, above the Double Happiness Noodle Shop on Rice Street. We have the top floor, so we don't hear the neighbors very often. We have large, airy rooms, and a bedroom for my father, one for the boys, one for Sokka, and one for Saqui and me—a great improvement over public housing. Plus we have windows on all four sides. We can feel the wind, winter *and* summer, but it is worth it. In the projects, you have windows on two sides, neighbors on the other two. You can hear every argument, smell every meal being cooked. I slept with one eye open, waiting for trouble.

My father doesn't understand why anyone would name this street Rice Street. There is no rice, except in the Asian grocery stores that dot it now. He shakes his head slowly from side to side, certain there is something he is missing, something he doesn't understand. I tell him it was named after a man named Rice, but again he shakes his head. A man named Rice? A man *made* of rice, perhaps, but *named* rice? No. And where are the bluebirds that are supposed to live in this apartment, he asks. There are only ratbirds—pigeons—and they are gray, not blue.

Not understanding is hard for my father. He respects learning, knowledge, and age. In Cambodia, as an elder, he would be sought out for advice, considered wise. He is always telling the children stories, and becomes sullen and resentful when they don't fully listen. Like this morning, over breakfast he told them the story about the mouse and the sparrow. A story I have heard many times:

It was a hot, dry summer. A sparrow flew across a river to find a mouse lying thirsty and hungry under a dead tree. She then went to find a cucumber and tied a string to it. She bit the string, flying and pulling the cucumber across the stream. When she got to the other side, she yelled to the mouse to crawl to the cucumber and hold on to it. She warned the mouse not to eat the cucumber because it was the only means to get him across to the other side and to get more food. By the time the mouse had floated to the middle of the river, he was very, very hungry. He forgot what the sparrow had warned. He started to eat the cucumber. One bite, then another . . . suddenly he found himself sinking into the water and the sparrow could not save him.

Sokka asked, while chewing her toast, why the sparrow had brought a cucumber. "Why not a stick to something else that floats that wouldn't tempt the mouse?" Sokka is the most thoughtful of my children. She can think her way around any question.

Hauly chimed in, "At least the sparrow could have chosen a food the mouse might not have liked."

My father pushed his chair away from the table loudly and said, "You children are like the mouse. Unwilling to take advice." Kor glanced up from his bowl of cereal, aware for the first time that anyone else was even at the table, with a startled look on his face.

Saqui glanced my way. She stood by the counter packing lunches, and she made it clear from her look that she was too busy to intervene. At home, I am in the middle of every conversation, the one trying to explain what someone else meant to say.

My father thinks Hauly should become a doctor. Kor would not make a good doctor. That we can all see. He is a daydreamer, hot-tempered and easily frustrated. His grades in school are average, at best. Besides, all he wants to do is play soccer. That and chase girls. Sokka would make an excellent doctor, and I keep telling her so, but my father doesn't think girls should be more ambitious than boys. It is hard for him that Saqui will become a nurse again, and make good money, whereas I will only be a translator. I do not have the memory or the means to get through medical school again. My work as a translator is important, even if the pay is low. I can bridge the gaps the elders in the community can't. I can help. I can make life better and easier for my people, for my community. So Hauly is to be the doctor. Problem is, Hauly wants only to paint.

He is pretty good with color. He has painted a series of watercolors of the animals at Como Zoo that are lovely and playful. He won an award at school for them. And he is now working on a series of oil paintings of the neighborhood. He has one of the Rice Street Grocery—the store itself no bigger than a grain of rice—paintings of our neighbors, their houses, their cars, their dogs, the bar across the street at closing time, all the people spilling together into the night. I take him to the art store on University to buy paints and canvas.

After the children had left for school, I found my father in his room, standing and staring out the window. He heard me come in. Facing the window he said in Cambodian, "I am like that elm out there. My limbs are dying. Too heavy to hold up. I am of no use to anyone. Not even the birds want to build a nest in me."

"Father. Don't you remember how I used to question you? The children ask questions because they know you know the answer. They are still trying to find it. The answer that is right for them."

"You are probably right. I am a silly old man, with silly old stories and sillier ideas about how children should listen."

"Only a wise man calls himself foolish." My father turned and smiled.

"And only a foolish man calls himself wise."

When we first arrived in St. Paul, Kor wanted nothing more than a television. Someone from the church gave us a small black-and-white one that Kor watched religiously. Cartoons and breakfast cereals, toys and slang he ingested, always wanting more. Sokka wanted a library card. Then she wanted to read every book in it. That was ten years ago, and she still spends all her free time there. She reads almost a book a day. Hauly roamed around the project picking up bits of treasure. Rocks and pinecones, dandelions and bird feathers. The feathers he kept in his pocket, in case someday he needed to fly. His world was full of fantasy, dense and impenetrable for the first couple years, but he too has found his way through. He draws what he can't explain, paints the world as he sees it.

I began work right away, quite unexpectedly. With the wave of Cambodians that filled the project we lived in, I found myself interpreting mail and forms for many of them, often accompanying them to various agencies. My education as a doctor taught me English as well, at least well enough to communicate what was needed. Pastor Olson came by a few weeks after we arrived and told me about the translator position through Lutheran Social Services. I jumped at it. Paid to listen, paid to talk. It was nothing like what I could have earned as a doctor, but that life, I already knew, was buried in Cambodia.

Saqui cried for the old me. We had met as students in medical school. She didn't think I should take the work. It was below me. All my education, wasted. She said Pol Pot had beat us after all. I tried to tell her that like the work, I too was a translation. That I still meant the things I did in Cambodia, but now I was understood differently. She argued that I wasn't a Christian, that this was a Christian organization. I tried to tell her that in America that didn't matter. What you believed and where you worked were separate things, unlike in Cambodia where your beliefs and your work were like your left and right hand. And it was something I could do, something *to* do. Even though I have never seen this Christian god with my own eyes, nobody at LSS asks or cares. It also meant money we could set aside to pay for her schooling.

I was lucky as a boy. My father set aside money, no matter how poor the crop, so that I could go to school. He said that he could see that there was no farmer in me. Even as a young boy, I found sitting and thinking more interesting than playing in the rice paddies. I studied hard and went on to college, then medical school. In 1972, I graduated from medical school, ready to work, and ready to marry Saqui. My mother said no. She wanted me to marry the neighbor girl, a kind but dull girl who was, according to my mother, a good cook—thus a good wife. We fought fiercely, my mother and I. Arranged marriages might have been fine for her generation, but they weren't part of mine. My father said marry Saqui, that if she was worth all this fighting, she was worth marrying. My mother came to the wedding but didn't speak to anyone. Which was not an easy feat for her. She loved to talk and brag about me, and I hate to admit it, but I kind of enjoyed her silence. By the time Pol Pot's regime destroyed all my papers and ended my career as a doctor, my mother had forgiven me and found Saqui's cooking to her liking too.

My mother died in Cambodia, right before we left for Thailand. And it is with sadness that I think of Cambodia and my mother buried there, alone. She had been sick for a while, but I'll always believe she knew what was coming, and couldn't bring herself to keep us from going. Father almost stayed when it came time for us to flee. I am grateful he made the trip—*survived* the trip—despite all the hardships it's brought him. For me, having him here makes my work as a translator more important. I can help him now. I can be his words. I can take care of him, like a good son should.

My favorite painting of Hauly's is of our next-door neighbors, the Larrsens, an elderly couple who have been in their house since 1945. We don't see them much in the winter. I worry about them. They seem so old, so fragile. Hauly watches their house from his bedroom window for signs of life. A light on at night, off by 9 P.M., a curtain opened in the morning, smoke from the chimney, exhaust from the furnace. We shovel their side-walk for them after it snows, and Mrs. Larrsen bangs on the front door, motioning for us to come to the house. We stand just inside the door, care-ful not to bring snow in with us. She gives me a cup of black coffee, and Hauly a cup of cocoa. The kind with the tiny marshmallows in it.

He has painted a picture of the Larrsens in springtime, hanging their laundry on the line, their pale skin like sheets, wrinkled and threadbare. There is new green grass in the picture, trees with buds about to burst, the wicker basket of wet laundry, the sagging clothesline and the weathered wooden pins holding Mr. Larrsen's undershirts, their towels and under-wear on the line. The sky takes up half of the picture, blue as a blue jay, with cotton-ball clouds dotting it. In the midst of all this is the Larrsens, looking like a wind could blow them away. They lean on each other. She in her housedress, he in his chinos and crisp white undershirt.

Saqui's favorite painting is the one he did of the library. In the picture it is built of books, solid and sure. Bricks made of books, and the window frames are words of advice—some my father has given him. And standing on top, like a statue, is Sokka.

He just finished a picture of the house around the corner, on Front Street. It is a duplex. Nobody stays there very long. The last people to move out left their couch sitting on the front lawn near the sidewalk. I thought the new renters would put it out with the trash, but no. They sit on it in the evenings watching the cars drive down the street. He has painted them at dusk, five bodies draped on that rain-soaked old couch, lit by their cigarettes and passing headlights.

This evening, Kor couldn't find his soccer cleats and I was helping him look. Of course the closet is the last place they'd be, but I thought maybe on an off chance, he had actually put them away. Tucked behind the shirts and jeans was a canvas, a painting Hauly had never shown any of us, of my father. In the painting, Father stands in a forest of greens—leaves and vines, mahogany trunks, and an indigo sky. He is surrounded by jungle animals, with a bluebird on his shoulder that is eating rice from his hand. In the jungle, the sky and the ground share the same space. Patches of color, patches of light. The horizon is difficult to see. Father's tongue is made of words. His eyes are clear and wise. I slipped the picture back behind the clothes, feeling like I had seen a human heart again, for the first time. It is an amazing organ, pumping, pumping, holding life in its grasp, following its own course.

Miini-Giizi

Miini-Giizi

NORA MURPHY

Arlington Hills

Lisa and I were cleaning up when someone knocked urgently at the door. We had been hoping to get home early and pack for the powwow down at Prairie Island. My niece looked up at me from the sink full of combs and waited to see what I would do.

"It's only four o'clock. If it's a customer, I'll take her," I said, leaning my wide-brush broom against the cash register.

When I opened the door, the sounds from the cars on Payne Avenue surprised me. So did the woman. She looked familiar—almost like I could see her dancing in the Grand Entry the next day. Her hair was long, straight, and brown. Her nose stood out from her face like my Aunt Delores's— proud and powerful. She wasn't Native, but I couldn't quite place her. Nor did I get a chance to. She started right in.

"I planned my funeral yesterday, I wrote my will this afternoon, and now it's time to get my hair cut. I take my grandbaby to Great Clips in Maplewood but my car's busted and I don't have change for the bus. Thought I'd walk up here and see if you ladies could help me out. I've got four cartons of blueberries. You can have half of them."

We just stared at her. She continued.

"I'd give you all of them but my grandbaby wants blueberry muffins and it might be the last time I get to bake them. Plus I just read a web site that says blueberries fight cancer."

I pointed to the first stall. The woman placed her tan plastic bag—the blueberries?—on the counter and sat down. Like me, she had to wiggle a bit to fit into the chair. I laughed.

I liked this troublemaker.

"Lisa, you finish up and go on home. Don't forget to take my dress out of the closet and you might as well put the sleeping bags on the front porch. Jerry will pick us up around seven."

I inherited the Silhouette Beauty Salon from my mom's sister, my Aunt Delores. It's a funny career for an Indian—so many of us wear our hair long or cut it off only when a family member passes over. But I love the challenge of helping people find their beauty. Some people say I'm good at it, too.

I got into styling hair because I used to work at the salon like my niece Lisa does now—only I used to help *my* aunt around the shop. My parents had had mixed success with their mixed marriage. I was half Anishinaabe and half Dakota. After Mom died, I decided to come up to St. Paul to live with my Aunt Delores.

I liked St. Paul, I liked my Aunt Delores, and I liked the Silhouette Beauty Shop. Eventually I got my cosmetology license at St. Paul Tech. Auntie and I thought we'd work together for years. But then she got sick and went home to the Rez.

Before Aunt Delores passed, she taught me her secret of beauty. "When you cut someone's hair," Auntie whispered, "You have to listen to their stories and find the part of their heart that each story holds. Then you need to match the movement of your tools with the secrets in their heart."

I know she was right. Beauty comes when you get the balance just right—the balance between the person's heart and the scissors in your hand. And when the beauty emerges from a person's face, it feels like you didn't even do the work—the customer and the scissors cut you right out of the scene.

I could tell that the blueberry woman had many more stories than I'd heard in a long time. I wondered if my scissors would know what to do.

"Are you from around here?" she asked as I wrapped the maroon plastic apron around her shoulders.

I liked this woman too much to get mad. Most Americans forget that Native people still exist. They would prefer to restore the prairies than actually talk to us. Last year, for example, the DNR planted native grasses on the south shore of Lake Phalen. You see, if *they* plant the seeds, they think they're still in control. Despite the popular record, Indian people are hard to keep down. We've always been here. We always will.

"I am—from around here," the woman continued. "The Barillas have been here for four generations—that's counting my grandbaby. My grandparents came here from Italy in 1920.

"Nona Barilla and his brother Marco worked at the Hamm's brewery. They also made their own wine for Sunday mass, feast days, and Nana's cooking. When Prohibition came, Hamm's had to switch to sweet syrups and near-beer, but the Barilla brothers kept on making wine and opened Barilla's Market. Do you ever shop there?"

"Nope, don't drink."

"Best discount liquors on the East Side."

"So how much do you want taken off—is this a trim or do you want to go short?" I interrupt.

"Real short. Real, real short. Then it won't be such a surprise when it falls out."

"All right then, real, real short," I repeated, combing her hair.

"Back then there was a code in this neighborhood. People stuck together. When the federal agents came around nobody told on anybody. But every once in a while the government discovered the bigger bootleg operations.

"My father remembers the time some agents split open Joe Vescio's supply. Rivers of moonshine ran all down Payne Avenue and into the creek."

"Back to the source, eh?" I asked.

"Yeah, ashes to ashes."

"Quite a family history," I said.

"My mother was Irish. She didn't want to marry an Italian because she knew they drank as much as the Irish. So when she was seventeen, she fell in love with a Swedish boy named Ricky Anderson. Every morning Ricky bought a sugar raised donut at the bakery where my mother worked. He'd watch her pluck the donut out from under the glass and bag it with a tenderness that he longed for.

"Every Friday morning Ricky would ask her out. And every Friday morning she agreed. He'd promise to take her to Phalen—to hear the community singings, to canoe around Monkey Island, or to picnic by the pavilion. But when Friday evening came around, Ricky never showed up. Instead, Ricky's friend Johnny Barilla appeared with a rose in hand. Johnny escorted Ricky's date to the concerts, the boats, the pavilion. When Johnny asked my mother to marry him at the Winter Carnival races the following year, she agreed.

"After they were married, my father finally confessed. On Fridays, the young men used to buy cheap cases of dented beer from Hamm's. My father would goad Ricky into drinking more than half a case. He would pour his own beer right into Phalen Creek. Then Daddy would drag Ricky to the back of Barilla's Market and head up Payne to meet my mother at the lake."

I had just finished cutting off the first layer of her long hair. The woman's head—capped with a jagged edge—looked a little like a blueberry still on the bush. We had just begun. To know what to do next, I leaned in to feel the shape of her head and to listen to the sound of her heart echo through her roots.

"Before you know it, I was the first Irish-Italian girl baptized at St. Ambrose. I remember my First Communion. It was on July 16th—the Feast of Our Lady of Mount Carmel. They still did the walks through the neighborhood back then. The men carried the Virgin Mother on a platform and the communicants walked behind the statue and the priests. Boys in black, girls in white.

"I remember how itchy my starched dress was. But I was proud. People taped money on the statue and they smiled at us as we paraded through the streets. I remember Mr. Vescio, the moonshine man—the one who lost his liquor down Payne Avenue—he was old then, but he waved at me with his cane.

"Mother didn't approve of all the wine that the men drank at the bazaar after the parade, but by then she'd become an honorary Barilla woman and couldn't say much.

"I'll never forget the mix of joy and sorrow in her eyes that day. The joy I understood—she was proud of me—but her sorrow didn't register until years later when I rebelled. You see, I *did* marry a Swede. I thought he'd be dry. Well, he wasn't. There I was with a baby of my own and no money to pay the rent. That was in the seventies and a woman could get divorced by then. Which is exactly what I did. I had had enough of men and their spirits controlling my destiny."

She paused for the first time, tapping her fingers on the armrest.

Then she said, "Sometimes I wonder if it's possible to outrun fate.

"What if Phalen Creek didn't run over the sandstone cliffs? Or if Theodore Hamm hadn't won the brewery in a bet against a bad businessman? What if my father hadn't gotten Ricky Anderson dead drunk and hid him behind Barilla's Market? Would I be sitting here getting my hair cut and facing death?

"I know one thing. My funeral will be a simple affair at Bradshaw's. No holy rollers up at the altar pretending they knew me. No hotdish suppers in a dark basement with Jesus staring from the cross. No caravan of people driving with a sense of duty over to Forest Lawn Cemetery. I will not be buried with my parents at Calvary. Not where Theodore Hamm's bones sit. He's had enough control over my life. Bradshaw's will cremate me. My son can take me home in a pot and do whatever he likes with my ashes."

A sweetness filled the air—released from the fruit hiding inside her bag on the counter.

"Where did you get the blueberries? Grow them yourself?" I asked as I feathered the crown of her head.

"Farmer's market. Hmong farmer. Funny thing, how they're taking over the area."

"They?" I asked.

"The Hmongs."

"Funny like when the Italians got here in the 1920s or when the English got here a few centuries before that?"

She ignored my history lesson and went back to the blueberries.

"I tried growing them myself. The soil's not acidic enough."

"My Aunt Delores said they used to grow wild under the pines near Phalen. But they disappeared when the city started messing with the water. I heard almost half of the lake disappeared."

"That's right. When I was a teenager, Phalen started to shrink. They built a retaining wall across the middle of the lake. Used to walk across it with my girlfriends. The lake was dry on one side and full of water on the other. Strangest thing. Sometimes you'd find things on the dry side—old wedding bands, pocket watches. Once . . ."

The woman wriggled in her seat and tilted her head back to continue talking. I gently pushed her head forward so I could finish up. We stayed quiet.

When I was done, I tipped her head back to center. We gazed into the mirror.

The woman looked more alive than she had when she walked in. Her proud nose still took center stage, but the shorter haircut showed off her high cheekbones. You could see the shiny flecks of green in her brown eyes.

She smiled for the first time.

"Well, isn't that something? Mr. Bradshaw's not going to recognize me when he throws me into his oven."

The woman picked up her brown bag and started to dig out the fruit.

"Do you remember the old Hamm's commercials on TV?" I asked as she set her blueberries next to the cash register.

"You mean the old Hamm's bear? Course I do. Why?"

"Do you know who painted that bear?"

"No. No, I don't."

"An artist by the name of Patrick DesJarlait."

"I see."

"Yeah, DesJarlait was Anishinaabe, from Red Lake, like my Auntie who used to run this place. I've got a copy of one of his paintings here."

I pointed to the Ojibwe language calendar on the back wall of the salon. Above the squares marked for July, an Anishinaabe woman wrapped in an orange scarf poured blueberries into a birchbark makuk.

The woman stared at the calendar. I looked into her eyes. Blueberries sparkled in her shining green flecks.

"Miini-Giizi," I said.

"Pardon me?" the woman asked.

"Miini-Giizi. Blueberry Moon. July."

A week later, the woman returned to the salon. She still had a full head of hair. She carried another bag. I could tell she was dying to talk. Lisa and I were both busy with customers.

"Looking for a trim?" I asked, looking at her from the mirror.

"No, I have a little something for you."

"Thanks, but can you come back at about two o'clock this afternoon—we're pretty booked up."

"Can't. Doctor's appointment. Well, I'll just leave this here. I found it when I was cleaning out the attic. I'm trying to get the house in order, you know, for my son and grandbaby. This must have belonged to the old Indian man who used to own my house."

I nodded and watched the woman leave. I couldn't tell which left a greater stillness in the store once she closed the door—her or the traffic outside.

It was one of those days. We didn't stop until after six o'clock. When we were cleaning up, Lisa asked me about the bag.

"God, I forgot all about it. Where is it?"

I leaned my wide-brush broom against the chair. The bag was on the shelf beneath the cash register. It was an old tan plastic bag from Cub Foods. I pulled out a small parcel wrapped in string. There was a piece of paper tucked into the package. It looked bulky—like someone had unfolded the paper once before, but was careless when they folded it back up.

"There's a note."

I read silently and then pushed at the string to open the package. What I found inside was a handful of hard corn seeds. I scooped them up and studied the colors. Mostly they were dark blue. A few were orange.

"Old corn seeds."

"Say what?" doubted Lisa as she stood up from her tub of combs.

"Look, it's old Indian corn."

"How do you suppose that woman got them?"

"I don't know. What did she say? She was cleaning out her attic, right?"

"An old Indian man used to own her house."

"But this note is dated July, 1975. Signed by a man. I don't recognize his name. It says he wants to pass the seeds on to the next generation."

"Why did they get stuck in the attic?"

"Who knows. Maybe he was forced out of his home."

I ran my fingers through the seeds. The note said the corn was from around here. Dakota corn, I figured. The seeds were hard, puckered. The blue ones reminded me of what Auntie said dried blueberries looked like in the winter before her mother soaked them in water. The deep orange ones looked like the Ojibwe woman's scarf on my calendar—folded and tucked with care. They were beautiful.

"My father's family would have planted corn like this. It's our turn now."

I didn't know the planting song for this corn. Not yet, anyway. I would ask the elders at Prairie Island next time I went down there. Yet I already understood one thing. The corn had its own story and my job was to listen.

My Friend Cíntia

My Friend Cíntia

DIEGO VÁZQUEZ, JR.

Sun Ray

My friend Cíntia says that since we both work the same hours during the middle of the night that we are both "cleaning ladies." "Sandra," she laughs, "the difference is that you clean offices and I clean out the wallets of perverts." I wish I was as good-looking as Cíntia. Well, I guess I am very attractive for a girl in my position. I just don't have the cojones to dance in front of a bunch of drunk horny men every night of the week. I always think I want to do it but then at the last minute I chicken out. Cleaning offices in the middle of the night in downtown St. Paul is a lot easier for me. The work is soft and quiet and sometimes I get scared but at least I don't have to deal with the sex thing.

I have a lot of time to think while I clean. One of my favorite spots is the Skyway branch of the St. Paul Library. I only do the library twice a week but when I am in there I must admit that I spend too much time reading books that somehow always lead to sex. In the middle of the night and me being the only person in this room full of books and what do I go for? I don't like to admit this to anyone, but I find myself wanting to do nothing but find research on sex. And no matter which book I pick up, it always seems to lead to my favorite alone topic in the whole world. I wish I had the cojones that Cíntia has . . . she works fewer nights than I do and she never has to work when she has her period. She makes so much money just for wiggling her body in front of men with wallets.

I don't know why I let Cíntia add to my name. I think she added the *Dandy* because I really don't have a middle name and she thought I should have one.

She insisted, "Mira, chica, you are more than just a *Sandra*. I think your stage name can be *Sandy Dandy*. That way if we ever dance together we can be the sister act of *Cindy Star* and *Sandy Dandy*, tonight, for your enjoyment."

I was only Sandra Gonzalez, that is with two z's in it, before my best friend walked into my life one night at the bus stop. She wore sparkles on her cheeks and her jaguar eyes lit the night with their intensity. Cíntia was taller than me and I am tall for a Chicana girl. I am 5' 6 3/4" tall and she has about two inches on me. Her dark brown hair was pulled tight into a bun but it felt like it was aching to spread out and flow down onto her shoulders. She had a wiggle that said she was important. She also did not look like a woman who often caught a bus. She certainly could not run toward one if she was late. Not with the high heels she was wearing. And those shiny black tights were just part of her skin—every curve below her waist, from her toes to her ass could be admired because of those tights. It was a cool evening in late September and she wore a small jacket that hid some very important parts of her anatomy. Later, after we became friends she would refer to her large breasts as, "these cows that are going to help me buy the farm."

The bus stop was in downtown St. Paul, across the street from Landmark Center and The St. Paul Hotel. Cíntia looked at me sharply with those wild cat eyes and she reminded me of an old dicho that my granny used to say, "If you ever see the eyes of a jaguar then you are already dead." Cíntia startled me with her quick eyes. I had to pay attention. She was loud and brash. "Does a bus stop here that will get me to Payne Avenue? To the Payne Reliever? You know where that is, don't you?"

And with those questions began a most wonderful friendship. I told her that I had heard about the Payne Reliever but that I had never really been there. I created a quick resume of my life to this point in my head. I have never been married and I will turn thirty in October. I live with my brother and his family and I like the arrangement because I rent the upstairs apartment over the garage that he built for me. We have lived on the West Side for as long as I can remember. And I know that hardly anyone from my part of town ever goes to the East Side. Unless some guys are looking for trouble.

I did go to college for two years but I stopped going because I followed a lover to Europe. Two years later I came back alone and determined to stay away from men for the rest of my life. So far I have done a good job. Tonight is almost four years since I have held a man in my arms. I have had a some-time-lover for the past few years but I do not talk about it. Especially to my family. I will never let them know my secret.

Although I am in love, it can't work out because my lover is married and she intends to stay that way. "Besides," she says, "Sandra, I can't leave my husband for a girl. What would my daughters think? Listen. I like what we have just the way it is. Dark. Secret. No one can ever know. And we just get together once in a while when we really need to be true to ourselves." I want to leave her because I need to live being true to my heart.

It has been three months since we have been together. Something always gets in the way, her schedule being much busier than mine. I don't have children; she has two small girls. I do not have much of a social life other than with my brother and his family; she is married to a lawyer/politician. She knows all the powerful folks in town; I clean for them. Yet I have fun by myself. I am a lonely artist who has been painting for as long as I can remember. Recently all I paint are watercolors. They are not what you see in the pretty galleries. The last one I did was of the kinder thoughts a woman has during her period. Magnificent colors. Most of my paintings are about thoughts and ideas instead of people or things. I have sold a few paintings but I am still very shy about displaying my artwork. I tell myself that after I turn thirty my resume will begin to look more like an artist's than like a mixed-up young woman whose career goal is to have cleaned every office in every building in downtown St. Paul.

That night at the bus stop, I remember telling Cíntia that I didn't even know if she was at the right bus stop. She looked at me and smiled. "Do you know what just happened? Well, no, how could you know. I mean do you want to know what just happened to me and why I am looking for a bus? First. I have no money on me. Do you see me with a purse? No. Second. I know you must think I am totally crazy and everything, but do you think I could borrow bus fare from you? I will keep your name and number and pay you back by tomorrow. Believe me. Listen, I am good for it."

I interrupted her quickly, "The bus fare is not that much. Yes I can give you the money. But, really, more important, what just happened? Are you in trouble? Are you in danger? Do you need more help? I can fight pretty good. My older brother and all of my older cousins taught me how to kick ass. Ha. Not really. But tell me what happened. And also let's find out how to get you to that Payne Reliever. Are you working there tonight?"

This is when I finally found out her name. "Perdóname. My name is Cíntia Estrella. At work they call me Cindy Star. And you are? OK, why don't we just catch a cab there together and I can pay you right away when we get there. I'll even give you enough to take the cab home."

"My name is Sandra Gonzalez with two z's. You know, this is good timing for you, Cindy Star, because I have just picked up my paycheck from work and I am not working tonight. It is Tuesday night and now I am thinking about going to a part of town that I never go to alone. And much less, I never thought I would go there with a total stranger. And another Chicana at that. Tú eres Chicana, que no?"

Cíntia laughed. "I got the abandoned part of me from a Chicano. The other parts are a bunch of green olives and some Navajo blankets and Tigua jewelry. I have pieces of Italy and the Southwest in me also. I am the product of what these days they call "date rape." My mother showed me the guy once but I never got a good enough look. Mom drove by at about a hundred miles an hour and about a block later she said to me, 'You know that guy back there? The one I wanted to run over? Well, that is your dad, but I could never prove it. So don't ever ask me about him again.' I was about nine or ten."

I replied, "You know, I was just reading a letter from my poet friend, Lilly Crista de Tejas. The Friends of the St. Paul Library brought her to St. Paul about three years ago and I went to hear her read at the Riverview Library. Her book is called, *My Lilly Is a Desert Flower*. I met her after the reading and we hit it off so well that she invited me to have drinks with her. It was wonderful. She is the first poet I ever met and liked. Since then I send her paintings and she sends me poems and stories. This new piece of hers sounds like it was meant for tonight. Can I read it to you while we wait for a cab?"

Cíntia wrinkled her nose, waved her hand across the sky, and said, "The only poets I ever met were as different as oil and water. I slept with both of them. Talk about strange ducks. They were really fun and smart and wild in the beginning, but after we made love they wanted to show me their 'poetic side.' One was so damn lonely and depressed that he begged me to marry him. The more I said no the more he drank. He finally passed out reciting some creepy poem about his eternal devotion to me and our love." She laughed and wrinkled her nose again. "The next morning the guy wakes up and doesn't say a word. He stares at me, at the wall, at his shoes, at my toes, at the door. He finally just gets dressed and walks out the door. Not even a good-bye. Never heard from the creep again either.

"The other poet was a longer affair but it ended just as goofy. I was actually starting to really like the guy and the more I told him this the more he began to think he was a really important poet. My heart didn't really count other than that he could write about it in some goddamn poem. Shit, I just wanted him to be a better lover. Then, just out of the blue he drops the good-bye on me. He says that he loves me too much, that I love him too much, and that it is interfering with his ability to be a poet. I told him he was full of shit. He said that as a poet he had certain rights that other people do not have, and that he had to leave me to better serve the world at large. He also mentioned that he thought it best that he remain with his wife and children. That was the biggest joke. It was not until he told me that he was dumping me that he mentioned his family. I feel sorry for them. So this poet friend of yours, is she as creepy as the men poets?"

"No. I don't think so. But then again we have never been lovers." Cíntia and I both laughed at each other until the taxi silently appeared. We jumped inside and I took out the letter from Lilly. I read aloud,

I want to go farther than the river. Maybe to downtown. Then, maybe I will catch a bus. It doesn't matter to me where the bus is going. Maybe it will go to Minneapolis. Maybe it will take me to heaven. But I want to go farther than the river. I come from a river on the border in Texas and now that I live In St. Paul, the West Side is not good enough for me anymore.

I see myself in each face of the new arrivals. I see myself in the tears of the tiny girls who already in their hearts carry the burden of our women. The small voices ask me how to find work. A chorus of sadness and joy at the same time. She will be stepped on for the rest of her life. She wants to find work. And her man is more than likely talking with his compadres about the need for revolution. About the need for changes. About the need to square this business of using the immigrants for the soiled rags and the clean rage of power of the well-to-do.

The small voice of the tiny girl whose heart is that of a woman in love has not yet learned the tone of the final agony. The final resolve that will forever separate her from the man she knew in the old blessed country of ten thousand miracles and ten million dreamers . . . her Mejico where her man was a boy searching for the heart of the most beautiful girl in the world . . . and where they kissed on the altar with the promise that all things would get better for them en los estados . . . and the wild promise on their wedding night . . . they will forever, the wild will of forever, the eternal kiss of forever . . . and the wild prometida . . . the most enduring prometida being that we . . . yes you and I . . . we . . . we shall stay together . . . through the hard times . . . through the birth of our children . . . through the ancient rebellion of a stranger looking into our window in the night when we make love for the first time . . .through all the hard . . . and through all the good . . . the prometida being that we two would stay together for-ever . . . and the voice of the broken heart so quickly and in the most unusual quiet known mostly to those who have been stranded in a burning desert after illegally crossing a border . . . in this most unusual quiet the girl begins to understand Freedom . . . and that the forever of a promise from her heart no longer matters as much as Freedom . . . so what in the world in estos estados is so miraculous?

This need for Freedom . . . and the girl listens to the directions from a woman who long ago abandoned love forever and accepted life in the States. Silent and argumentative she returns to the last conversation with the love of her life . . . he saying before leaving for war that, "You cannot live en los estados and expect to love the same person. It does not happen with freedom. If I die you will need to address this issue."

All she remembers is tickling his belly and laughing at his attempts to sound professorial . . . he promising not only to love her forever but to return from the war and go to that college in California that had already said that he could attend . . . and she remembering that upon his return he would study to become a professor, and life ever-so-complicated would become ever her most favorite garden . . . a garden where she would plant the flowers of each of her three children . . . they laughing together before he left that he would barely have enough left in him by the time they would need the third child . . . and they both knowing before he left for the war that he would return with sad eyes, but that he would return to the promise of their forever . . . a forever which started on the night of stars in the old country when the farmers cried and the city people laughed at the eternal beauty of storms that sing with the stars.

When I finished reading Cíntia sighed, "Well, loca, it must be time to cross the river. I think you should hang out with me tonight. Besides, I still haven't told you what happened downtown. And you've got to hear this story."

The cab driver asked if he should wait and I told him no. I looked at Cíntia as if she should hold my hand and I whispered, "Will it be OK?"

Cíntia told me to relax. "Sandy Dandy. Look, maybe we could get you on stage tonight. Just kidding. But sure it will be fine if you hang out with me. I will tell them that you are thinking about joining the business. Believe me, girl, as long as you're with me everything will be fine. And I really don't have to be here very long tonight. I just have to get some money and do a quick shift and then we are out of here. I like you, Sandy. So stop looking so scared. Lighten up, girl, I won't tell anyone in your family that you were here."

I started to get nervous, but I realized that I felt calm and safe with Cíntia. "Oh, you are funny. I couldn't care less who knows where I go. Yes, I am a little shaky about doing this, but as Lilly said, *I want to cross the river.*"

"The Payne Reliever on a Tuesday night is just as crowded as it is on a Wednesday night. There are no empty seats," Cíntia said to the stars and then turned to me. "I don't even count the faces anymore. Sometimes I am up there and all I see is one big face. One big smile. One big tooth. One big eye. One monster. And I dance to keep the one monster happy. It pays well when the monster is satisfied."

Inside the dance club Cíntia walked up to a man and began to speak rapidly. The man listened and moved his eyes around the entire club in constant motion. Cíntia finished speaking to him and walked away with a handful of money. She walked over to me and asked me to put the money in my purse. "Sandy honey, hold this for me. I still don't have a purse and you still don't have my story. Come with me while I get ready for my number and I can tell you all about it."

In the dressing room, Cíntia started to tell me the story, but the interruptions were too many. "This man from Iowa who comes into town every other week became a good friend. Well, I believed that he was from Iowa. His name was Ned Smith. I should have known that no one is named Ned Smith . . . it was an alias. I like Ned. Well, I liked him better a few hours ago. I'll tell you the rest later, dear, there is too much going on here."

Cíntia and I were surrounded by naked women in that messy dressing room. She looked calm and peaceful and happy. They should hire me to clean the dressing room, but I don't think they could pay me enough. I think I would just redecorate it and give all of the girls private space. And I retire from office building cleaner lady to dancing office girl? No, you look too serious all the time. We would have to train you to laugh and also to pretend that you are enjoying the laughter. But we would have to get you to smile first. When was the last time you smiled for longer than a second or two? Ha. Probably at someone's funeral who you didn't like. Yeah. That's what you do. You probably are only happy with revenge. Are you a vengeful girl? I'm sorry. I am getting scatterbrained. I need to get you a cab. You know, I have enough money in your purse to buy a car tonight if I wanted to. Hey. We got all night. Let's take a cab to Lake Phalen and look at the moon over the lake. We can have the cabbie wait for us. And then we can go eat somewhere. I need to see the moon over the lake right now. OK?"

Cíntia did not have to convince me to do anything. I was about ready to follow her to the goddamn moon itself if that was where she wanted to be. "You are funny. Sure. I got nothing but time. I wish I had someone to love. I got a purse full of money that belongs to a woman who was a complete stranger three or four hours ago. Now this complete stranger is trusting me to carry her cash. Sure, Cíntia. I think this night is ready for me and I have certainly been waiting for a night like this. I just didn't know that I *was* waiting. Hey, you're not from the West Side, are you?"

Cíntia pulled a taxi out of the night sky like a magician pulling a rabbit out of a hat. We were already inside the cab when she answered me. "Why does everyone in the Twin Cities automatically assume that if you got Latina on you then you must live in the West Side? I know Mejicanos who live in Shoreview. Hell, I know one who lives in Minnetonka and another who lives in Shorewood. Guess what, girl: Mejicanos are everywhere. I have a friend from St. Paul and he always goes away for months at a time to work in Alaska. Anyway, once he told me a story about la migra even catching a whole bunch of illegals out in the Alaskan bush who were working for a power company. They hauled away the entire work crew—about forty guys—and then the whole area was without electricity for a long time. Yes.

We are everywhere. And even if we are legal, it still feels illegal being Mejicana up here. No. I do not live in the West Side. I was living in Shoreview before I left the boyfriend. Now that I am homeless maybe I will consider moving into St. Paul. I sure like the town a lot better than Minneapolis. It feels more colored to me."

I found myself smiling for longer than two seconds and Cíntia caught me. I laughed loudly and tried to talk. "Cindy Star / she will go far / because she doesn't have a car / but she has enough cash / to make everyone kiss her ash."

Cíntia laughed with me. "Oh, no! Not another goddamn poet in my life! Though it sounds like you are the best of the bunch."

We landed at Lake Phalen and Cíntia told the cabbie to find us a spot close to the water. And to wait for us because she wanted to show me how to skip rocks. The cabbie nodded his approval. We walked to the water searching for flat rocks on the beach.

I had an idea and I decided to blurt it out. "Cíntia. Tonight, whenever we decide to go home, I want you to come home with me. Stay at my place. Check it out. I have a spare bedroom. You might want to become my roomie. The rent will be very reasonable."

The moon bounced across the dark, calm water. Its reflection caught Cíntia in a warm, soft hesitation. She breathed deeply and sighed, "Are you sure? We just met. I am a stranger. A dancing girl. A girl who has money in your purse for having done a favor to some people who can get very mean. I have never lived on the West Side. But I would love to come over tonight. Let's sleep on it. I mean, wow. Thank you."

The search for flat skippers took a long time. Finally we got to the water's edge. Cíntia twisted her arm and wrist like she really knew how to skip rocks. Under the moonlight her flat rocks skipped and danced on the water and demanded the attention of everyone around her. The rocks were like her dancing. Each toss became more magnificent than the others. "Sandy. Do you want me to show you how to toss them?"

I did not tell my new friend that my brother and cousins taught me a long time ago how best to toss rocks across the water. I learned so well that I could make all of them look silly in any competition. But this was no competition. And I could never make a rock dance on the water. That is for Cíntia alone. What I have seen skipping under the moonlight in the longest smile that I have ever known is the new trail that will take me and my best friend all over the world.

A Working History
of the Alley

A Working History of the Alley

JOANNA RAWSON
Hayden Heights

Begin with the alley at twilight.

Say it's high summer. The heat-dull air is shot through with pollen. Strays interrupt the heaving down of the air into evening—a chorus of their kind rising to a distant siren.

Southward: the river, still wild. Upward: ancient light sprung from a trap of exploding stars that's finally arrived.

And all around: the city, doing what machines and music do.

Along this block-length stretch of alley, crickets pulse in the ribbongrass that insists its way up through cracks. The patch of blowzy cosmos camouflages a snack-chip wrapper it snagged from yesterday's storm, both oranges caught in the shadow of a moth-spattered back porch light like tatters of fire. One garage door is riddled with bulletmarks. The next, behind a small eatery, with graffiti and the traces of last fall's crazy hail. Down by the corner, the rust-ripe chassis of a scrapped truck thirsts for another fix of rain. Its sunburnt iron perfumes the undulating air.

Begin here, in this story's one-night stand. Imagine it an inscribable surface. An invitation to doings. A convergence, say.

Believe this could be about anywhere, until the figure of a child furiously pedaling a royal blue bike turns from the street and into the alley, specifying it by this sudden presence, hurrying toward us and in so doing setting off each motion-detector floodlight in passing, like a succession of emergency flares, so that the contraption of rubber and chrome appears to be flying in parallel with a speeding blaze. From here at the other end, the child appears no bigger than a crow, illuminated in silhouette by the fires.

A man sits on his back stoop, twenty feet from the alley. His shoulders are bowed and crooked, as if most of his body's career has favored the left. We see that his chest is thin under a sweat-soiled undershirt, that his posture suggests calcification and the accumulation of grief. Liver spots mottle his hands' parchment-thin skin. The knuckles have been seized by arthritis and his left hand holds the fixed shape of a claw. He leans in, this elderly and ill-lit man, closer to the precarious metal tabletop perched on a stump by the cement step and taps his spectacles into the rut their weight has carved from his nose.

Notice the shaking in his wrist as he cocks a whittled pencil between forefinger and thumb and begins to write, whispering lead into the surface of a sheet of very white paper. His lips move as he reads along with his writing, and so appear to be giving his hand dictation.

"Greetings, Jozef Rozwidowski," he writes, in his native Polish. "After such a long while (six years, is it?), to receive your letter yesterday was indeed a welcome moment! I'll have you know that I have not forgotten that particular meadow of golden blooms you mention, and yes, how we boys used to run through them until we were gilded with pollen from tip to toe at about this time of year. Little did I imagine that on the other side of that idyll lay a killing field, and now there is an ocean and nearly sixty years between me and that paradise.

"Because you have amused me with this memory, I enclose for your delight this Agence France-Presse photograph I have clipped from our local newspaper here in St. Paul. You see that Baska the Horse, after thirteen years of hard labor in the Wieliczka salt mine—426 feet underground, no less!—has finally been hauled up to the light and retired to a fine green pasture. A well-deserved rest, I would say.

"To which I must add, my dearest Jozef, that I too am coming to my own rest. It will be tonight, and done by the time you receive this reply. It is true that I have known my mind has been going for several months now—softening! melting!—and it is a relief to me, an old gray horse myself, to have the presence to take my own life while I am still sound.

"Why this decision? Let me simply say, although it is not a simple thing: I do not wish to be alive after I have forgotten the ordeal you and I and all the others suffered together in the camps. What with the lapses and blurs and lengthening fugues of late, it could be only tomorrow that this forgetting occurs.

"To have lost in memory that smell of mortal smoke or the cold heaps of shit or the weak rattle of our skeletons bickering about bread and God—well, should these stories vanish from my skull, it would be as if those years had never occurred at all. I exist in terror of this. I tell you, sometimes the fear that I will utterly neglect to remember these events makes me wonder if perhaps one's history is even more ephemeral than I have so far suspected.

"What if I should pass the moment when I become unable to save myself from this oblivion? Capable only of reporting what it was I had for breakfast or how many moths flickered above my porch light, as they do here tonight (by my count, six)?

"Or consider: being too far gone to shuffle through my cerebral cortex and locate the story of these faded numbers along my forearm the next time a stranger at the corner grocery should touch them and ask. Can you imagine? The answers are too bleak to countenance for yet another day, my old comrade."

At this, the man's scribbling ceases. He lifts his gnarled left hand from the page and begins to knead it with his right, working blood back into the tips. Because the future is as unpredictable as the past, he mutters, because it may or may not be that luck or grace or the authorities intervene, the wind kicks up and turns the wildfire from its fatal course, the squall dies down and spares the capsized boat its fate against the palisade reef, the bullet lodges in the hostage's irrelevant appendix, the airborne car lands upside down in a swimming pool, unscathed, because even now, after all this time, the ashes to the east blow and feed a meadow of perennial goldenrod their daily sustenance—because we cannot say with any assurance how the story will go . . .

When the first true pain hits, Pepita, as they call her, is tending to the thriving patch of serrano chiles she's installed in one of the twelve bald car tires that have found new life as planters in the hardscrabble yard behind her uncle Felix's taquería. She's brought the seeds from her hometown of Ciudad Alvarez. The odor of the ripening foliage and the stings of the little fruits' incendiary pips on her fingertips make her homesick for the old streets. When the next contraction seizes her belly, Pepita tucks her scissors into an apron pocket, crosses herself in the waning twilight, and doubles over against the chain-link fence bounding the alley. "Sí," she whispers in Spanish to the baby who last Sunday fiddled itself into launch position in her pelvis and since then has been hiccuping and sparring with her spine. "I am waiting for you to burst into this world. Come along, little rocket."

She sucks in shallow breaths just as the manual that she and her husband Ernesto got at the nearby clinic instructed, and pictures the effect as that of scooping crescents of cool melon from a rind. Pepita can hear the radio playing banda in the kitchen where just an hour ago she'd helped her uncle scour the grill after the last dinner plate had been served. A patina of grease and sweet onions still slicks the stagnant evening air. The useless fan her Aunt Inez propped against the screen door clicks out a steady cadence to which Pepita hitches her breathing, in counterpoint to the crickets' pulsing in the alley.

Her uncle glances out the window just then and catches a glimpse of her raven hair twisted into a bright yellow scarf and her thick body sagging against the mesh fence. This is how the women in this family labor, Felix thinks—their ample butts slumped over their bent knees and sweat running in rivulets along the fine down of their necks. Qué bonita. He'd accompanied his wife through it five times in a bedroom upstairs. The midwife and the other women had tried to shoo him out with Carlos, the first, some twenty-six years ago, but he'd insisted on staying put with the boiled water (shouldn't someone always boil water for a birth?) he'd hauled up in the pozole pot. He'd stationed himself in a straight chair in the corner all night and smoked—two full packs, sharing a cigarette with his wife when she wanted the nicotine to soothe her—until the baby's vernix-streaked head crowned into the pool of lamplight and the rest of the room's population yelped and wept. Later, each time Inez discovered she was pregnant, she would announce the news to her husband by placing an ashtray on the bedroom chair.

Felix nods and turns from the window. "Inez!" he calls into the dining room, where a few dinner stragglers are still visiting over crumbs. "It's time."

Sweet bitter corridor, constitution of quartz and lime: history hurries down the alley. Bits of its residue stick to the juts like the silks proud poor old men wear to tatters. Sucker birches woven up through the cyclone fence list and quiver. In the pursuit of happiness a crippled squirrel plucks at a crib mattress crumpled in the dumpster. Bats circulate among the strung live wires.

The child, a boy (we can tell now, by his cropped hair, as he approaches on the bicycle), could not care less what goes on around his frantic expedition. He's in a state of propulsion. If you knew where he is going, if you knew what he is going for, believe me, if someone were to tell you the entire truth of what put this boy on this mechanism and wound them up into motion, if this terribly small person were to suddenly brake and skid to within reach, lean in to whisper "I've been waiting for this night my whole life . . ." and it spilled from his mouth into the dark like a deliquescent shadow, you might not be able to exist in exactly the same life again.

So as not to overdose, let us, his audience, his authors, bring him down the alley in slow-motion, the spokes spinning in rhythm with the crickets' insistence and flashing silver glints where the detection floods catch. Let's switch him to a track that takes a measure different from real time to arrive—like the death-light of stars—and feed his hot tires and his very heavenly body through the thickened urban firmament gradually, so as not to hurry the story beyond its native capabilities.

In the meanwhile, a common spider continues her colossal web that stretches from the phone pole across the alley to a busted gutter. See how it clots with the ephemeral wisps of spindrift this heat strips from the spent cottonwoods and uses to shroud the slaughtered flies strung there, in midair.

Night has fallen so far with the old man inside it, what's left to locate him is only the sound of his pencil gathering speed against the rough page. That, and the weak porch bulb strung naked on a cord and mottled with the perishing wishes of moths. Picture him crouched within the hush. The breeze is picking up. Its rising undercurrent carries now the whiff of honey, which reminds him.

"My old comrade Jozef, tonight it takes the odor of this sweet air to grant some levity to my situation. Leave it to the bees to spread cheer around with such abandon! As I have written in previous letters, the gorgeous perfume of new honey (almost sickening in its intensity) can turn any place, no matter how humble, into an arcadia. Above any other sensation, it is the one that remains supreme in my recollections of childhood there in Pelow.

"Perhaps when I began my little hive of Carniolans here behind the lilac hedges I believed it was simply to resurrect my long-lost beekeeping skills and to get enough harvest for an autumn's worth of sweetened toast. (Their stings also proved to be quite the panacea for my arthritis.) I consider now that it may have been for no other purpose than to manufacture this redolence of propolis and honey, by the industry of these insects, from flowers translated at the height of blooming.

"For the first time since coming to St. Paul so many years ago and setting up this backyard operation, I let the colony fall into neglect this spring, which means, I suppose, that I allowed the bees to revert to their true nature, without any human intervention to thwart their desires. They swarmed, as I knew they would. They threw off their winter torpor. The workers laid siege to the crocuses and hellebores like a band of frenzied muggers! I found the budding virgin queens all plumped up on their royal jellies by the time the apple blossoms were out, eight of them in all, and I simply left them to their own devices. In the days before the colony divided, I could hear rumors of supersedure in the change of their collective vibrato emanating from the hive at daybreak. The disturbance was unmistakable, even though I hadn't heard such a thing since I was a boy.

"They swarmed on a Thursday. I witnessed the exodus from my kitchen window, as the black cloud lifted from under the lilac and funneled up to the route their scouts had determined. I could understand their elation, of course. They were gone in an instant, off to stake their claim elsewhere in the free world. Their chronicles are not so unlike our own, my friend—of the glorious mapping of that wilderness beyond the known hive, swollen with sustenance and hazard, and then its conquering and taming down into a livable dwelling. How like us these myopic bees are, after all, constructing cities from elemental glue and dreams, sustaining them on civics and need. What empire! What intrigue!

"Elka used to cluck at such notions. Many times as we sat on this stoop together, growing old and brittle as two sticks, I would while away the evening with my grand theories of the divine order ruling this social world of humans and *Apis melliferas*, of the unified field of entropic inevitability which began in a garden and will end, again, in one of eternal verdant delights, and so word by word and image by image, as if climbing a ladder of rhapsodic utterance, would reach the moment in my waxing when she would lean in and pinch me hard on the shoulder blade, right where she surmised my wing would be attached had I one, and cluck. 'Stasio,' she'd say, 'you are like a bee drunk on nectar. Stop your waggle-dancing. Stop this foolishness. Come back to earth!'

"Seven months now since my Elka passed. The bruise on my shoulder remains. It appears to be permanent, after all those years of pinching. I may well be cursed with a tattoo on my forearm, telling a tale of horror, and blessed with a tattoo on my wingblade, telling one of love."

By the time Inez has cleared the last of the dishes and gone out to fetch her inside, Pepita has pitched to the ground and crawled on all fours to the trunk of the mulberry tree by the gate. There she arches and begins a signal of low moans that rise and fall as she alters her squat. How gorged she feels, like a sated tick. A sudden spurt of liquid trickles down her thigh.

In the lull between waves, Pepita attempts to convince her plural body to let go its firm hold on her mind and allow it to drift up to a more aloof position from which to marshal the pain. At the next contraction she vomits into the understory of milkweed, rousing a nest of monarchs to flurry up into the evening's last shaft of blue light casting through the canopy of leaves. The expulsion seems to do the trick, and the young woman's mind, too, hikes through the wing-stirred air and perches on a low branch.

It is from this spectral vantage that Pepita watches Inez exit the kitchen and hurry toward her body crouched in the weeds. Around her the tree teems with starlings flocked to the rotting fruits. She pivots and peers across the alley at an old man sitting on his back stoop, rocking gently with his eyes closed. His bearing reminds Pepita of her grandfather, who'd first hatched the notion of crossing into the United States to have her baby, and so deliver it into citizenship on its first day on earth, as her cousin and another young woman from her town had done.

The evocation sends Pepita into a reverie, free as she is from all aching up there on her limb in the summer ethers. She trains her gaze toward the end of the block, out the blind alley, past White Bear Avenue, and into the distant heat-warped skyline of downtown St. Paul. And then, with an apparition's spectacular acuity, she finds herself able to spy across the sweeps of sweet corn and clover ribboning along the Mississippi River, southward over the sunflowered plains and sienna flats and alluvial swamps and then into the baked broken earth where the Texas-Mexico border runs like a badly stitched seam. She sails into the mountain-bounded plateau of Zacatecas, moving back, back through time into each successive horizon that in her delirium vanishes in a chimera of steam, and brakes her flight above her native Michoacán state, where her feverish vision alights at last in a remote village nestled between arroyos, which tonight appears to be dreaming in a like-minded heat.

Pepita watches as a young couple emerges from one of the dwellings, a man and a woman, he toting two satchels, she obviously pregnant and off-kilter at the hips. They walk to the road where a black pickup idles. The open palm stuck out the window takes their folded bills and signals them into the back. The pair climbs in, the driver revs the engine and shifts, and the truck lurches once, catches, and commences the trek north. From there time doubles back, and Pepita's hallucination traces the forward chronology along the Sierra Madre to the borderlands around Ciudad Juarez where a coyote shuttles the undocumented immigrants across by night to the bus station at Albuquerque. It is another several days to the terminal in St. Paul, where her cousin greets them with a bag of tamales in one hand and a Polaroid camera in the other.

In the snapshot Pepita appears bewildered, as if she's just been spirited through some freak rip in the space-time continuum, squinting against the glare, laden with child, an instance of starlight escaped from its original detonation.

To venture through. To exit the main commotion and find passage. To turn a corner and enter into the inner reaches of the city's gridwork, into the determination of this order stamped onto wilderness, and be given access to the flipside—the houses and shops and eateries with their public faces fixed elsewhere—through which this alley snakes and straightens, pocked by ice cycles and heat spells, trafficked, hollyhocked, an archive of trysts, truants, quarks. The alley does not shine its boots. It does not shave or cope or oblige. Its panic is not the dreamed-up kind of the highway. It is an evacuation track, at the end of which, for the boy, the end of time ticks.

He wheels past the third house in, the empty lot across from it. He is making progress—a point of view advancing into the crux. His breathing narrates a plotline. Inside the house a woman is scanning an online auction's list of 45s for that old song—how did it go? something about what?—she wakes up to sweating every few nights remembering it as the soundtrack playing at the exact moment the telegram arrived, thirty-seven years ago tomorrow. In the rubbled-up vacancy across the way, a pitched-out scorched couch with a curse of corroded springs for cushions turns itself into shelter for the couple of teens knotted together in a lust they can't even pronounce, though its motions creak and hum. You could shake a story loose from every building and every absence along the way. He doesn't mind any of them, desperate as he is to arrive home.

We see by the triggered glare of a safety light that the pedaling boy is barefoot and dressed only in a pair of denim cut-offs too large to properly ride his hips. A smear of mud decorates his chest above one nipple, and the grass stain across his ribs looks like sheer green gauze stretched over a toy washboard. He has been playing, which on his body looks as much like violence as joy, and lost track of time.

Here, I'll let you in on a secret: The boy is flying home to meet his father. His father, the boy's father, and the boy—they've never met. Why?

It's a long story, as they say, and what they mean is that truly saying it would take the time the story itself took—real time—to occur. For now, just imagine: A summer night not unlike ours. A man, two months from becoming a father at age nineteen, just off the late shift at the plant. A bar—family-owned like most around here, two beers on tap. There couldn't've been more than a dozen men in there that night. The overhead fan was going but the air in there was beyond hot, stifling. Even by last call it hadn't cooled to reasonable, which had turned everyone's nerves on edge. August 29, 1993. Two days before payday. Some wiseacre backs up from the pool table to line up a shot and jabs the man, who is perched on a bar stool facing the game, in the ribs with his stick. It could be a mistake. The two had traded words earlier, but it could well be. Even so, the man, with his son in the making, takes it as provocation and hurls himself onto the player's back. The fight takes less than ten minutes to finish. Later, in court, the exhibits included the pool cue, two teeth, a series of photographs shot at the hospital and the medical examiner's office, a recording of the 911 call, and the murder weapon. The father, which he was by the time of the trial, forbid his new wife from bringing the baby to the courtroom. So as not to see him like that, he said, shackled there to the table or under guard in the visiting room at Stillwater during the nine years afterward. He attended the anger-management sessions, during which the killing worked its way out of his gut like a shag of shrapnel. He paid reparation. He planned his release into the outside. He called home to talk to his wife but couldn't brook hearing the voice of his son, whom he called Tiger, which sounded in his ear too much like chiming on the moon. So he wrote to the boy, who as he grew up began to write back.

"Dear Daddy, tonight I went with mom to her work and we vacuumed the hallways and waxed the cafeteria floor and then took a break on the roof to see Mars."

"Dear Daddy, Uncle Stephen told me that during the Viet war you got a little monkey for a pet and trained it to open the fridge and drink beer and one day it got too drunk and croaked, is that true?"

"Dear Daddy, I will be home to meet you when the parolers let you out on Sunday and have a cake party in the kitchen. Here is my school picture so you will know me."

"Jozef, the hour is late. I have run nearly to the end of this sheet of paper. God willing, you will be able to decipher the script of an old and tired man— chicken scratches, as they say here in my adopted Midwest, scribblings in the abyss, hieroglyphics. I must close, as I have other, final work to do.

"But bear with me a last moment (with the price of postage these days, I hate to leave any white space unmarked). What I told you about mem-ory—the failing of mine, and the fear—is true, yes, but there is a bit more to it. I recalled the other day the small bottle my grandfather filled with his mourning tears in the days after he was widowed. It was a blue glass, bril-liant in the light. On the day of her funeral, he corked it with a dab of wax, placed it in the casket (between her breasts, I recall) and buried it with her.

"Why do I remember such things? That is a mystery. Why do I tell such things to you, to my own dead wife, to strangers at the corner store, to this sheet of paper, to the wind? I suppose it is in order to let my words deliver the memories from their private hiding places and out into the world. Perhaps to charge the grunts and melodies that come off my tongue with meaning, and to launch these into the ears and eyes of another—for no other reason than safekeeping.

"My decision that this be my life's last day came when I realized that with Elka gone (she must be glad to have at last escaped my frivolous musings, and will be somewhat annoyed when I arrive to pester her with them in the beyond!) I have no one left to deposit my stories with. I have lived in this neighborhood for how many years? It seemed I used to know everyone by name and among them there were intimate friends, more than one of whom considered me a hero for fighting with the resistance, once they heard the tale. True, that sort of familiarity is not always pleasant—in fact it grows tedious to hear for the hundredth time about Mr. X's kidney stone operation (twelve he pissed out, one the size of a robin's egg) or Mrs. Y's secret for prize roses (strands of chest hair she'd plucked from her sleeping husband, sown around the roots). Still, we traded these stories in a world of stories, and because of it I was someone.

"Now I am no one. This is a lonely affair. My city block has changed into a place of strangers who rarely stop to speak as they pass down the sidewalk, or cross the alley for a visit. For instance, who can I tell this little story I stumbled across yesterday in my reading? In 1810, Lorenzo Langstrothborn, an aspiring seminarian and inventor of the modern hive, was struck with hysterical voicelessness before giving his first sermon. He turned, in desperation, to beekeeping. This saved his life, but it did not free him from sorrows. For the balance of his days, despite the delights of his vocation, Langstrothborn suffered from spells of melancholia, during which he could not bear to be within sight of his hives or even to look at the letter B!

"I ask you, who? And who might care to surrender an anecdote from their own singular drama in exchange for one of mine? This is the commerce that binds us together, friend, and without it I am afraid that we are all—"

And as the old man stops his pencil and fine-tunes his feeble wrist to scribble the next word onto the page, he lifts ever so slightly the index finger of his right hand which has been anchoring his suicide note to the makeshift table, and the breeze, steadily rising since dusk and promising a thunderstruck midnight and rain by dawn, reaches in under the page and raises it into the air where just beyond the author's fingertips a honey-edged current snags it and spins it upward and across the yard, airborne, twirling in a dervish of wind toward the threshold between the low-watt light and the darkness, into which, in another instant, it vanishes.

The old man, swatting his stiff hands about and stirring up a storm of moths, stands and shuffles over to his cane leaning against the rail. "Oh, to hell with these aching knees! To hell with this wind!"

His muttering, as he hobbles toward the alley, sounds like the hum of bees.

"Pepita? Pepita?"

Her aunt kneels down beside her in the yard and loosens the buttons along the back of her dress. "This is no time to be proper," she says. "Your foolish uncle has seen it all before, bless his soul. He's gone to boil water and fetch his chair."

Inez had come from the kitchen to find Pepita down on all fours with her eyes glazed over and wearing a vacant expression. She was growling like a guard dog, as was the habit of Diaz women in labor, with diluted blood smeared over her legs and feet like a pair of sheer stockings. Inez recalls The Birth Plan (a three-page document) that Pepita and Ernesto devised in the month since they arrived, after studying too many library books with titles like *Special Delivery: How to Guarantee the Birth Experience You Want* and *It's Your Baby: A Postmodern Couple's Guide to the Miracle of Labor.*

They intended to produce an all-American baby according to correct methodology—a well-adjusted newborn and, most crucially, a u.s. citizen. Pepita's husband still has but a limited command of English, so Inez figured that perhaps the key concept regarding reproduction—that God laughs at our plans—had been lost in translation.

Felix parks the chair on the back walk. "For Ernesto," he says to his wife, "heir to the throne." Ernesto and Carlos had driven off in the family car that morning because on Sundays the bus doesn't run to the job site. They aren't expected home until well after dark. Felix unwraps a fresh pack of cigarettes and lights one. He appraises the two women for a moment—a stranger might easily mistake what is going on in their hot little huddle for some sort of violence, a mugging or an assault—then shifts his attentions to the mulberry tree above them, a gnarled, weathered thing that erupts cacophonous birdsong at each rustle of rising wind and in the dark seems as mysterious a phenomenon as what is in the works below.

"Old man," Inez calls over her shoulder, "get your head out of the clouds and be useful! This girl is about to bust open. We must get her out of these weeds and into the hospital. Go call the ambulance!"

Felix nods and goes inside, past the cauldron of lukewarm water on the burner. "Ah well," he murmurs, "perhaps I could boil up some chicken later." When the dispatcher answers, he gives the address and says "My niece is having a baby in the backyard. Please, por favor, come through the alley."

The boy has pedaled close enough now for us to hear his winded breathing. His chin cocks as he registers the nearing siren, which has set the neighborhood strays into a keening chorus. Even before it turns into the alley he can place the ambulance by its emergency lights streaking the sky above the rooflines and erasing the low-slung stars. Is it about my father? Has something happened to my father?

Still cursing, Stasio shuffles to the corner of his garage and ducks his head out. His wayward letter, a pure white stamp on the dark, rustles and darts on a spiral of wind, eluding his reach as it careens past, flattens against the fence, then gambols away as if drawn by the banda music playing on a radio across the way until it is drowned from his hearing.

At the first shriek of the siren Pepita remembers herself and leaps from her perch in the tree back into her convulsing body below. She feels wildly disoriented, as if the red flashing atmosphere were some sort of bloody and contracting womb giving birth to her. Inez takes shape beside her and then Felix, unlatching the gate for the paramedics as he announces that he'll follow them to the hospital in the car with Ernesto when he gets home. The foliage beneath her cheek is cool and smells like the iron in rain. As the emergency vehicle pulls up and parks in the alley the baby presses against her spine, with its fontanel at the threshold of the world.

The boy looks up suddenly to see the ambulance door swing open into his path. He skids and swerves left, colliding with the airborne letter. It snags in the spokes of the bicycle's front wheel just as the old man lunges for it, his limbs akimbo and a grunt fired from his chest, so that all he sees in the midst of his precarious waltz is a blur of chrome and wheeling legs before the door hits him and he clutches it to halt his fall as his final dispatch spins off into the dark. Pepita tips over onto the stretcher as directed and feels herself rise in a nest of i.v. tubes and sensors and levitate toward the portal of the ambulance that the old man she recognizes from across the way seems to be holding open for the occasion. " Gracias," she whispers.

And just as suddenly, the drama is over. Felix and Stasio, left alone together in the still wake, watch the taillights proceed down the alley, turn, and disappear. The two glance over at one another and nod by way of greeting. "Good evening," the younger man says. "Good evening." The moment, and another, ticks past. Then, "My name is Felix Diaz. Thank you for your assistance. In all of this commotion I seem to have forgotten to eat dinner. Would you care to join me?"

The old man acknowledges the offer with silence, until, with a barely perceptible uprising in his shoulders, he turns toward this stranger, clears his throat, and says, "My name is Stasio Kolyszko. Yes, yes I would like that," and allows himself to be guided by the elbow toward the lit kitchen of the taquería.

And later, after the reunion, as the boy lies in bed with his nerves jacked up on sugar from three pieces of cake and the free lilt of his father's strange voice in the yard outside, he will turn on his flashlight under the sheet and study the beat-up letter handwritten on very white paper that he has retrieved from where it stuck to the spokes of his bike, and its indecipher-able script, thick with jammed vowels and odd accents, will seem to him a sort of mystic communication from the beyond, saying what he can't yet divine, though in time he will suspect it of being true confirmation that the last words he whispered tonight into his father's ear were right.

WRITE A BOOK IN YOUR COMMUNITY

Write a Book in Your Community

Twelve Branches: Stories from St. Paul developed from a simultaneously grand and simple concept: let's write a novel at the library. The project, as it developed in St. Paul, took many turns before publication of this book. But it had three important goals throughout: to promote use of the public library, to involve many community members in the process of writing, and to produce an outstanding, enjoyable book of fiction.

How did we plan and implement this project? And, how can other communities replicate this model? The project involved three distinct phases: an extensive planning period; writing workshops and community involvement programs in the library branches; and finally, taking the written drafts of twelve chapters through the editing, design, printing, and publication of this book.

Partnerships were key to this project. As the lead organization, The Friends of the St. Paul Public Library organized a small planning group to oversee the project. The group included representatives from Friends staff, board, and committee members, as well as from the library and Coffee House Press. We received excellent advice on working with writers from COMPAS (Community Programs in the Arts), an organization that provides writer-in-residence programs in schools throughout Minnesota. Early on, the planning group realized that funding and publicity would be crucial elements of success. Publicity for the project was coordinated to coincide with publicity and programming surrounding the reopening St. Paul's Central Library following two years of renovations. Our local daily newspaper, the *Pioneer Press*, provided a generous commitment to support the project with a series of free monthly ads. Funding for the project came from The Friends' own programming funds, and the receipt of a significant grant from the Anna M. Heilmaier Charitable Foundation. Later, Target Foundation also provided grant funds for the project.

The planning group made a number of crucial decisions early on. First, we would hire professional writers to lead workshops and write the final stories. Next, the project would visit each library branch for a one-month residency. Finally, the format of the published book would consist of twelve, neighborhood-based works of fiction. Our original concept of writing a novel with one writer was abandoned both because we felt it would be too difficult to carry the storyline from one library branch to the next, and it was more practical to hire three or four part-time writers than a full-time writer for six months. We also realized that tapping into the talents of more writers would give the book a greater diversity of voices, reflecting our changing community.

We advertised in local literary magazines for writers. We looked for individuals who were both accomplished writers, and who had experience in teaching or leading community writing workshops. Our interview committee emphasized the need to find writers who could work with a variety of individuals, as well as produce first-rate, publishable stories on deadline. During the interview process, we discovered the need to find a balance among the writers' teaching experiences and styles, as well as find individuals who would work well together.

In February, 2002 the writers began visiting branch libraries for one-month residencies. Two writers were active every month, and each ultimately worked at three different branches over the six-month period. At each branch, an opening reception was held early in the month, followed by four workshop-style programs scattered throughout the month. Displays were also set up in branches where community members could learn more about the project, and forms were provided for contribution of story ideas without having to attend a program. Stories and ideas were also accepted via an e-mail address, publicized on both the public library's and Friends' web sites. At each branch, the writers also worked directly with one or more school or community groups to gather stories from the surrounding neighborhood. Teacher packets with suggestions on how to contribute to the project, developed with the help of the writers, were distributed to local schools. Through all of these activities and programs, the writers gathered plots, characters, and anecdotes to capture the local flavor of the neighborhood and library branch.

As might be expected, each writer worked in a slightly different way. One focused on having people tell stories of any kind, whether fact or fiction. Another conducted informal writing workshops, while a third had individuals focus on neighborhood history. The fourth writer engaged attendees in conversation to elicit tales and plot ideas.

The community participation phase provided the greatest challenges in the course of the project. We learned anew that the neighborhoods of St. Paul are quite diverse, and participation in the project varied widely from site to site. Our expectations for attendance changed quickly. We expected one hundred people to get involved at each branch, but attendance was about half that. Still, at the conclusion, nearly 500 people participated in the creation of this book. Despite extensive media coverage, community involvement depended most heavily on word-of-mouth promotion by library staff. Most individuals greatly enjoyed the process once involved, but we learned that many people were initially intimidated by a project focused on writing. Without altering the intent of our programs, we quickly changed our promotional message to the "sharing of stories." Some misconceptions about the project, most commonly that story submissions would be published verbatim or that this was going to be a nonfiction work on neighborhood history, persisted. Finally, it was difficult to maintain energy and enthusiasm over the entire six months. When we repeat the project, we will do so in a two- to three-month period with fewer programs and workshops. Despite numerous lessons learned, the community phase of the project overall was successful and rewarding in terms of publicity, participation, and the contribution of story ideas.

Publishing a book requires skills and talents not found in most community organizations, and working with an established publisher was invaluable. At the close of each month's library branch residency, the writers were given a deadline of two months to provide a story draft for that branch. The stories were edited for content and continuity by Chris Fischbach, the senior editor of Coffee House Press. Layout, design, and printing were also overseen by Coffee House Press. Working with a professional, experienced publisher was crucial to the success of the project. Not only did the project have the benefit of expertise in the practical aspects of editing, publishing, and distribution, but working with an established publisher allowed us to attract more accomplished writers and garner more publicity throughout the project.

The *Twelve Branches* project required an unusual amount of effort and resources. Any library or organization replicating the project should carefully consider and plan for the level of resources appropriate to their community. The basic idea of the project—*writing* a community book—has the potential for being even grander, or much more limited, as resources permit. For instance, working with one writer to create one new short story with community input is manageable for most communities and organizations. Regardless of scale, the St. Paul project provided powerful confirmation of the value of conducting a *Twelve Branches*-style project. Our successes included: the participation of nearly 500 community members in a writing project; providing support and recognition for local writers; the development of ongoing relationships with community partners; the opportunity for staff enrichment in working with creative artists over an extended period of time; significantly increasing awareness and use of the public library; and the publication of an exciting, new form of fiction. The project, while not without challenges, proved a huge success for the library, the Friends, and our partners. With the publication of *Twelve Branches,* the project once again returns to the community. The published work will endure for many years in the library and hold an important place on participants' and readers' bookshelves. The publication will be celebrated with community readings and events throughout the St. Paul Public Library system, once again multiplying the impact of the project.

Our hope was to produce a widely enjoyed book and to contribute to the creation of good writing. We think we have accomplished our mission, and we are proud that the foundation of *Twelve Branches* is rooted in the evocative stories of the people of St. Paul.

Stewart J. Wilson
Director of Public Awareness and Communications
The Friends of the St. Paul Public Library

The Friends of the St. Paul Public Library is happy to support the creation of projects similar to *Twelve Branches* by other libraries or community organizations. For additional information on the *Twelve Branches* project at the St. Paul Public Library, contact Stewart J. Wilson or Andrea Moerer at (651) 222-3242 or Friends@TheFriends.org.

Acknowledgements

The Friends of the St. Paul Public Library and Coffee House Press gratefully acknowledge the generous support of the *Twelve Branches* project by the following organizations:

Anna M. Heilmaier Charitable Foundation
St. Paul Pioneer Press
Target Stores and the Target Foundation
Irwin Andrew Porter Foundation

Additionally, *Twelve Branches* was made possible through the ongoing support and guidance of the staff of the St. Paul Public Library.

∼

Coffee House Press is an independent nonprofit literary publisher supported in part by a grant provided by the Minnesota State Arts Board, through an appropriation by the Minnesota State Legislature, and in part by a grant from the National Endowment for the Arts. Significant support was received for this project through a grant from the National Endowment for the Arts, a federal agency, and the Jerome Foundation. Support has also been provided by Athwin Foundation; the Bush Foundation; Buuck Family Foundation; Elmer L. & Eleanor J. Andersen Foundation; Lerner Family Foundation; McKnight Foundation; Patrick and Aimee Butler Family Foundation; The St. Paul Companies Foundation, Inc.; the law firm of Schwegman, Lundberg, Woessner & Kluth, p.a.; Star Tribune Foundation; Marshall Field's Project Imagine with support from the Target Foundation; Wells Fargo Foundation Minnesota; West Group; Woessner-Freeman Family Foundation; and many individual donors. To you and our many readers across the country, we send our thanks for your continuing support.

Special Thanks

The Friends of the St. Paul Public Library thanks the following individuals and groups for their willingness to contribute stories and ideas to the creation of *Twelve Branches*. Thanks also go to the many anonymous contributors to the book. As a living entity, St. Paul is the sum of your stories. With your help and through your stories, we hope *Twelve Branches* has captured a snapshot of our city.

The *Twelve Branches* project was conducted over six months. Despite our best efforts, we recognize that we may have inadvertently overlooked a contributor or managed to misspell a name. Please understand that any errors are unintentional and accept our apologies in advance. Thank you.

Lou Adams
Denise Alexander
Astrid Anderson
Becky Lee Anderson
Luke Anderson
Michele Anderson
Oralee Coopie
  Anderson
Shardae Baker
Patricia Banks
Melissa Barker
Jeanneane M. Berger
Mary Bjork
Coreen S. Blau
Jacqui Blue
Margie Boler
Elvina Buckley
Ann Bulger
Katie Burns
Cambodian Elders
  Group at Christ
  Lutheran Church
Beverly Carroll
Victor Chow
Carly Christensen

Adrean Clark
Kathleen Clark
Kathy Clark
Mary Leah Comer
Ben Dansky
William E. Davies
Michela Dimond
Virginia Dischinger
My-Trang Ngoc Do
Liz Donohue
Michael J. Doyle
Jennie Duchschere
Mel Duncan
Lawanna Edwards
Carol H. Egan
Oda Eiane
Colin Erickson
Orville Ethier
Pat Ethier
Taylor Evangelist
Linda Fleming
Barbara Friberg
Jesse Fylstra
Katie Gentner
Jenna Glass

Cynthia Glover
Orpha C. Goodhue
Ruth Gould
Eleanor Graham
Helen Grams
Georgia A. Greeley
Rose Gregoire
Floreen M. Hagen
Mai Nhia Hang
Sigurd T. Haugan
Shelly Hawkins
Lenief Heimstead
Bee Her
E. Young Her
Mong Her
Jenny Hill
Bunny Hollibush
Anne Holzman
Gary L. Hovey
Katherine Howard
Renie Howard
William A. Howard
Doris Allen Howe
Dominique Hudalla
Galina Ivanova

Ramona Jacoboski
Mathew Jirele
Miss H.M. Tiny
  Johnsrud
Wellington Jones
Emily Jorgensen
Norm Kagan
Patricia Keefe
Dan Kelley
Jean Kivel
Karen Koeppe
Patricia Krezowski
Dina Ky
Heather Pekarek Kyong
Chris Lain
Zack Lameyer
Laura L. Lanik
John Larson
Marguerite Lee
Pernilla Lembke
Chia Neng Lor
Deng Lor
Sonja Mee Lor
Deborah Love
Sergio Lozoya
Timmy Lubke
Nicole Lunda
Carmen M.
Dorothy L. MacKenzie
Eva Madison
Scott C. Magnusen
Don Mains
Barbara Malas
Ruth Sampe
  Mammenga
Reece Maranda
Tanya Martin
Carol Martinson

Marietta McCullough
Suzanne McGinn
Ann McKinney
Merrick Community
  Center Seniors Group
Judy Miller
Samantha Miron
Allison Moncrief
Mai Yia Moua
Patty Mullen
Cate Murphy
Wahdatullah Nazari
Megan Nickelson
Amanda Nielsen
Mary O'Briend
Maria Orme
Modupe Osunlana
Bonnie Palmquist
Anne Elstrom Park
Karen Kolb Peterson
Iglika Petrova
Justin Pieliowski
Joey Powell
Sue Pummill
Elizabeth Putzier
Mark Rawson
Matt Rayburn
Vera Reznikova
Jack Rossbach
Margaret Ryan
Jon Rydel
Anita Rylander
Mary Ann Sachs
Brittany Sargent
Christine Schendel
Mae L. Schmidt
Greg Simpson
Barbara Sommers

Britney Starks
Lisa Steinmann
Lucy Steinmann
Crosby Sommers
Ginny Stavn
Polyxeni Syvertson
Beulah Swan
Shannon R. Swanson
Dennis William Szondy
Toua Thao
Isiah Thomas
Marjorie Toensing
Betty A. Trepanier
Emily Turi
Kim Tyler
Alan W. Uhl
Tsuj Fum Vaaj
G.G. "Frenchie" Vadnais
Jack Vandrachek
Andrew Vang
Cher Vang
Shoua Vang
Janet VanTassel
Caitlin Varhalla
Doua Pao Vue
Ze Ger Vue
Sarah A. Wadsworth
Carole Waltzing
Andrea Weidling
Brent Williamson
Stewart J. Wilson
Wilma Wilson
Betsy Winterer
Rose Wright
Pang Yang
Fred Zachau
Ramona Zamora

The Friends of the St. Paul Public Library

Peter D. Pearson, President

325 Cedar Street, Suite 555

St. Paul, MN 55101

(651) 222-3242

www.TheFriends.org

St. Paul Public Library

Randy Kelly, Mayor of St. Paul

Gina LaForce, Library Director

90 West Fourth Street

St. Paul, MN 55102

(651) 266-7000

www.sppl.org

Libraries

Arlington Hills
1105 Greenbrier Street, 55106 (651) 793-3930

Central Library
90 West Fourth Street, 55102 (651) 266-7000

Hamline Midway
1558 West Minnehaha Avenue, 55104 (651) 642-0293

Hayden Heights
1456 White Bear Avenue, 55106 (651) 793-3934

Highland Park
1974 Ford Parkway, 55116 (651) 695-3700

Lexington Outreach
1080 West University Avenue, 55104 (651) 642-0359

Merriam Park
1831 Marshall Avenue, 55104 (651) 642-0385

Rice Street
1011 Rice Street, 55117 (651) 558-2223

Riverview
1 East George Street, 55107 (651) 292-6626

St. Anthony Park
2245 Como Avenue, 55108 (651) 642-0411

Sun Ray
2105 Wilson Avenue, 55119 (651) 501-6300

West Seventh
265 Oneida Street, 55102 (651) 298-5516

Bookmobile
(651) 642-0379

Please Note
The Skyway branch, which served downtown St. Paul,
closed in late summer, 2002, to prepare for the reopening
of Central Library on October 5, 2002.

THE WRITERS

NORA MURPHY

Nora Murphy is the author of two books for young readers, *A Hmong Family* (Lerner) and *African Americans in Minnesota: Telling Our Own Stories* (Minnesota Historical Society Press), co-authored with Mary Murphy-Gnatz. Her articles have appeared in *Minnesota History, A View From the Loft,* and *The Circle.* Murphy has also written and edited works for many community organizations, including the Minneapolis American Indian Center, the Hmong American Partnership and the Chinese American Civic Association. She has an MFA in Writing from Hamline University and an undergraduate degree from the University of Chicago.

JOANNA RAWSON

Joanna Rawson is a poet, journalist and creative writer. She has taught writing at the high school and college levels, and has worked with many diverse groups of writers, including prison inmates, American Indian teens, and senior citizens. A long-time staff writer and editor for *City Pages,* Rawson is also a member of the *Rain Taxi Review of Books* board of directors. She is the author of a collection of poems, *Quarry,* and has also published more than 200 articles and reviews in *Salon, Utne Reader, Mother Jones,* and other publications. Rawson holds an MFA in Creative Writing from the University of Iowa Writers Workshop. She has received a Minnesota State Arts Board Fellowship, and awards from the Minnesota Newspaper Association and the Society of Professional Journalists.

Julia Klatt Singer

Short-story writer Julia Klatt Singer is a rostered artist for both COMPAS and the Minnesota State Arts Board, working as a writer-in-residence in schools across the state. She has published over thirty-six short stories and poems in various publications, including *SLANT*, *Buffalo Bones*, and *Women's Words*, and edits the online journal *writeworks*, which features the writing of her students. Her writing has won awards from The Loft and *Rambunctious Review*. Singer has an MA degree from Hamline University and an undergraduate degree from St. Olaf College.

Diego Vázquez, Jr.

Diego Vázquez, Jr. is a poet and novelist. He is a writer in residence through the COMPAS Writers and Artists in the Schools program. He is the founder and former Slammaster of Slam MN! (Minnesota Poetry Slam). Vázquez is the author of a novel, *Growing Through the Ugly* (W.W. Norton), and the editor of two COMPAS anthologies, *Rooftop Jailbirds*, and *River Pigs*.

Good books are brewing at coffeehousepress.org